Martina J. Kohl – **Family Matters**

Martina J. Kohl

FAMILY MATTERS

Of Life in Two Worlds

PalmArtPress
Berlin

"Life in a Frame" was previously published in Kohl, Martina. "Life in a Frame." *American Studies Journal* 67 (2019). Web. 2 Mar. 2021. DOI 10.18422/67-06. This book includes a revised version.

The quote prefacing this book is from "The Beginning of the End of the Beginning" in *Black Dog Days. Poems by Brian Burt*. Georgetown, Kentucky: Finishing Line Press, 2022.

The two framed pictures from *Life in a Frame* were kindly photographed by MemoWerk, Eltville am Rhein.

ISBN: 978-3-96258-134-3

All rights reserved
© 2023 PalmArtPress, Berlin
All photos: © M. J. Kohl
Edit: Ulrich Kempkens
Cover: Michael Apitz
Layout: NicelyMedia
Printed in Germany: Schaltungsdienst Lange, Berlin

Palm**Art**Press
Publisher: Catharine J. Nicely
Pfalzburgerstr. 69, 10719 Berlin
www.palmartpress.com

In the spirit of sustainability, this publication was printed on FSC-certified paper in a climate-neutral manner.

because nothing will ever be
the way it used to be
& anyway was never
the way it was
to begin with

from "The Beginning of the
End of the Beginning"

                      by Brian Burt

To Anna . . .

ONE – Preface
Born in Manhattan — 9

TWO
Life in Frame — 15

THREE
Little Henry — 46

FOUR
Clara — 61

FIVE
Little Henry II — 89

SIX
The Bay Window — 114

SEVEN
Do You Like Honey? — 144

EIGHT
When Everything Changed — 172

ONE
PREFACE
Born in Manhattan

I was about ten years old when I discovered an old passport in the attic of a 300-year-old farmhouse that my grandparents owned and where I lived until we moved into our new home at the other end of the village in Germany. The attic was a creepy place for us kids, yet full of wonders. Old crates from overseas travel contained my mother's hand-made carnival costumes, like Queen of the Night and the cowboy and Indian outfits my brothers, my sister and I loved to wear and which were inspired by Winnetou and Old Shatterhand movies. The expired passport, stuck between discarded documents in a cardboard box that was hidden among the costumes, belonged to my grandfather Heinrich, whom everybody called Henry. Upon closer inspection, I noticed that it listed his birthplace as New York – a fact I had never heard about, a topic that simply was not an issue within my family, something everybody knew but took for granted. So, it escaped us younger kids completely.

I had attributed my grandfather's love for "Amerika" to the fact that my aunt, his youngest child, had married an American G.I. after the war. She had moved to Omaha, Nebraska in the late 1940s. A framed photo decorated with a little American flag above his small, red velvet sofa showed her wearing a fashionable scarf and dark sunglasses in front of Niagara Falls. Apparently, she travelled a lot. My grandfather was extremely proud of his daughter. She had gone back to the land of his childhood and lived a life he might have envisioned for himself.

Together with his mother, Henry had returned to his father's birthplace at the age of nine, roughly my age at the time I discovered the passport. On a visit to the homeland, relatives had talked his father into coming back, leaving behind a supposedly very successful tailor shop on the Lower East Side in exchange for his father's shop in the old farmhouse in a small village close to the Rhine river. People there still had their clothes made by a tailor, at least for a few more years, until the big department stores selling mass-produced clothing, which had threatened his Manhattan business before, were taking over the business in German towns as well.

Henry's mother, the German-born daughter of immigrants to New York, did not want to return to a village which offered her nothing but the status of an outsider.

Yet, she did not want to give up her only surviving child, the youngest of nine. So, she sold everything in Manhattan, took leave of her mother, father and siblings whom she would never see again, boarded the *Pennsylvania* together with Little Henry and eventually joined her husband. It must have been around 1907.

She could not take much with her, but the big plywood crates that were still in the attic some sixty years later, filled with our things, not hers. She must have cherished two large paintings, though, with ornate wooden frames that depicted a young couple in front of a lavishly decorated wedding bed, and the same couple supposedly nine months later with a baby in her arms. Both husband and wife reflect a respectable, comfortable, yet formal life. We still have these portraits in my family, the only items left from the New World, or her German household, for that matter. I often wondered if her life had been anything like that in far-away New York. I don't think she had a happy life in that little village with a husband who spent more time in the pub than with her. She died in her forties, and it might have been a precursor of the Spanish flu that took her and her father-in-law's life within weeks of each other. She was never spoken of, her name forgotten, as if she had not even existed.

Henry's fascination with "Amerika" remained. In his bedroom, he hung his mother's two framed pictures when he married the daughter of a widow from the neighboring village. Henry claimed he was still an American citizen and got away with it during late recruitment for WWI, when he most likely still was, and again during mobilization of the older men for WWII, when he probably wasn't an American anymore. In 1945, American troops occupied the Rhineland, and, finally, the untrained laborer received some recognition, had a skill nobody else had, because he still spoke the language of his childhood. He was able to supplement his small family's income with goods from his American friends who accepted him as one of their own. Many villagers were envious of his good relations to the occupiers who would become allies eventually.

Language is power, so Henry helped save the baker's car from being confiscated by the U.S. army, the only car in the village which would be needed if somebody had to be taken to the hospital. And he got his factory boss out of the de-Nazification mill. He would not have to worry about losing his job from then on. What Henry and his wife Katharina worried about was their son. Not even 16 when the war started, he only re-joined his parents after three years in a prison camp in Croatia in

1948. His sister by that time had grown into a young, radiant woman, had made friends with the GIs she met through her father and left home for America to marry one of them.

Like many women of that generation in the western part of Germany, she had become fascinated by the Americans stationed in her region who were so different from the young German men who had gone to school during the Nazi years, learned to walk in step but not to question, and returned traumatized from the battlefields and prison camps to find everything they were made to believe in ruins. They pushed their memories, traumata and atrocities they had seen or committed out of their minds only to be captured by them in old age again, after the work of rebuilding Germany had long been done.

The following stories, in FAMILY MATTERS, are fueled by the lost stories and voices of some of these relatives, especially the women, some of whom have left few traces, sometimes just a name or a photograph. They did not keep diaries or leave behind letters. The stories reimagine their lives, give them a fictional voice, take them out of these sepia-colored photographs and place them in their own time. They make them come to life. The stories span several generations, stand on their own, but connect through family ties and one person at the center: Little Henry. The underlying theme is the fascination Germans have had with a country ever since its founding, a country that eventually influenced Germany more than any other after the war through its soldiers, pop culture, and its promise for a better future. And, as this introductory chapter indicates, this book will also be about my own fascination with "Amerika."

TWO
Life in a Frame
1907

Two large wood-framed pictures, that's all she was able to bring back on the boat. And a couple of oversea crates with linen and clothing and a few photographs. *Bring back?*

She had no recollections of the old country that she and her younger sister had left as toddlers. They still spoke the Swabian dialect with Mama and Papa, but the East Village was their home and English her and Clara's preferred language. You could pay her parents, and they would not go back. They had done well, invested the money from the sale of their bakery in a Delicatessen, and when the business grew, so did the apartment they had all lived in together then, away from the tenements. She loved her busy neighborhood. Though it felt like a small town, the East Village connected to the large landscape of the big city which was full of promises and dreams. And yet, here she was, packing her life up into a couple of oversea crates.

Should she even wrap up these two big, heavy wood-framed pictures? They would take up so much space, and the glass might even break on that long journey. Mama and Papa had given her the first picture when she got married to Henry, and the second after Lilly's birth, her beautiful little girl. Lilly whose grave she would never visit again, her parents whom she was leaving behind as well, and Clara, her sister. They had become somewhat distant after her marriage, and when Clara started to travel so much with her lady orchestra, they hardly saw each other.

Mama and Papa valued a good education for their girls, and her sensitive brown-haired sister had been allowed to take private music lessons. After hearing Camilla Urso play, the famous French-born violinist, when she was only ten years old, Clara could not be stopped. The summer she finished school, she had asked Papa to enroll her in that music school with a pompous name: *National Conservatory of Music in America* on West 25th street. They admitted female students, even Blacks, amateurs and aspiring professionals. First Papa had hesitated. But since the Conservatory did not charge tuition, he had given his consent. How proud Mama and Papa were of her disciplined musical sister, though playing the violin was still considered not exactly lady-like; and how hard Clara had worked, practicing every day for hours. But it paid off: She joined a group of female musicians and turned into a successful violinist, just like Camilla Urso, or almost. And now Clara even earned money, her own money, by touring the country with this famous female orchestra. Her sister got to see the hustle and bustle elsewhere. She missed her, but there was also slight envy in her heart.

She herself was not very musical, but she loved to draw. As a girl, she had often wondered if she was as gifted as Clara. It was the hustle and bustle right here, in front of her house that had inspired her sketches, the market stands, the people, the horse carts driving through the busy street. She had dreamed of traveling to draw what was beyond the big city and often walked down to the pier to sketch the boats being loaded and unloaded. There it was, even today: the promise of future travels to far-away places, a promise only partially, and ironically, to be fulfilled soon. Then the world was coming to her, all the immigrants pouring into the city, connecting with communities and family already here or venturing off to go west. She had spent hours putting her sketch book together and thought about enrolling in art school. If only she had done so, she thought when wrapping the photographs of Little Henry in her linen towels. Going *back* might apply to Big Henry, but certainly not to her. And yet, that's where she was going together with Little Henry, to *Big Henry's* village. She had no choice.

What would she have done, she wondered, if she hadn't met Henry? Papa had known him before she did because they sang in the same *Gesangverein*. She had first spotted him when they performed at one of the neighborhood festivals. His bright blue eyes, the waxed mustache and the way he wore his hat slightly tilted to the right, his well-tailored suits and dimpled boyish smile on his round face still made him a favorite with the ladies, though he now was a bit heavier, his hair a bit thinner. Back then a group of factory girls had been standing in front of the band stand trying to draw his attention. But he had only looked at her. Henry loved music, had a deep voice, carried the tune faultlessly. He was one of the leading voices of his choir. Their eyes had met, and Henry had made sure to be introduced to her, Elizabeth, his fellow choir member's beautiful daughter.

Big Henry posing

Henry had arrived from the old country a few years before, all by himself. He had left in kind of a hurry,

18

he said, because he thought he had killed somebody in a beer brawl. Insults had been exchanged when his temper took over, a temper she had not witnessed during their courtship, but later during their marriage. This hot wave of anger which surged right out of his belly into his head. He had hit the other boy hard, too hard. He wouldn't get up. Henry recalled that he had panicked, run home, grabbed a few things and made off on a Rhine bark towards Amsterdam, and then on to America. He almost hadn't had time to say good-by to his mother, the only one who really cared about him, who called him *mein Schatz*, still did in her letters, which she found odd because he was a grown man.

Henry was a good storyteller. He had described to her the slow boat trip down the Rhine valley taking him further than he had ever been, painfully reminding him of the beauty of the place: green vineyards clinging to the slate rocks, small rivers feeding the old stream, medieval castles topping impossibly steep cliffs, and eventually fertile flat fields giving way to the North Sea. She had made some sketches as she imagined the scenery he had described, just to make him happy, because even then in their courtship days, she had sensed that Henry was a torn person, adventurer on the one hand, deeply rooted on the other like the vines on the hills around the old village. He could have gone back. A few months after he had found a place in New York, a letter arrived from his folks urging him to return: The fellow had not died after all, they wrote. But by that time Henry had become fascinated by the big city. He made friends easily, had found a job in one of those numerous little tailor shops before setting up his own, and shared a place with one of his colleagues nearby. Before he had met her, he would roam the streets of Manhattan on Sundays, walking all the way to that bridge built by a German whose name he had forgotten and which reminded him of gothic church towers back home. He had often wandered up to the big park built to allow the city folks access to some nature, and he still did sometimes. There, he would sit on the grass and dream about going back home to the Rhine valley as a rich man and show them all, eventually.

Elizabeth folded the bed linen and Henry's night shirts and placed them carefully on top of her own.

What had she seen in him back then when he had courted her? A free spirit, no doubt, somebody who expressed his opinion strongly and became the center of attention quickly. He had a fine sense of humor, was a charmer. He had called her Lisa with a soft „s" the way it was pronounced in German, brought her flowers and sweets and a beautifully embroidered shawl. He had made her laugh with funny stories about his customers, and had often talked about the future when he could afford a trip home, just to see if his folks were doing well and to show off to the farm boys. Maybe they could go there together, he had asked.

Henry was a talented tailor, and because he had been lucky to come with a modest sum provided by his father, he did not have to start at the bottom in his new city. He had been smart enough to scout out the neighborhood, talk to the local business owners, and when one of the stores was listed for rent in his street, he had managed to set up his own shop. John, a young man from Ireland he had befriended, had joined him. Henry was the boss, of course, and they both had worked hard, still did, but knew how to have a good time as well. Henry enjoyed being part of the German immigrant community with its all-male choirs, sports and bowling clubs and crowded beer places. This was his link to the old home. And this was where they had met during a neighborhood festival.

She had loved spending time with him. She remembered that Papa had liked the young German but thought him a bit irresponsible, especially when Henry had had a few beers and entertained them with tall tales and witty remarks. Papa had not been too keen on welcoming Henry into their family. When Henry's kisses had become more passionate and his hands too busy under her coat, there on the park bench in the dusk, she had pulled back—reluctantly. Mama had warned her to be careful. So she had told him what any good Catholic girl would say, that she would only give him what he wanted if he was serious about her. Maybe she just had wanted to test him, she wondered. Just to find out how deep his feelings were for her. She remembered being a little surprised when Henry proposed. But by that time, she had deeply fallen in love with him.

Hadn't she talked about going to art school?, Papa had asked. But he could not talk her out of it, nor had he tried too hard, because he had never seen her so happy. Nothing had seemed more important at the time. She had been ready to embark with Henry on the biggest adventure of her life, a life full of passion and love, maybe travels, too. What a romantic she had been. For a while she had forgotten about art school and her envy of her studious sister who was wedded to her beloved violin. At least she would get married, have a family of her own, be the daughter who would give her parents grandchildren, something Clara would not, she had told herself.

Maybe the narrow escape after the beer house brawl was just one of Henry's tales he had made up to entertain her, she wondered when placing a few of Little Henry's toys in the crate. Maybe he had simply escaped the boredom and poverty of his village. The future there was entirely predictable, and progress expressed itself in plans for train tracks running through the small main street of the town to connect the train station three miles south with a fashionable spa three miles north. Trouble was the train, small as it was, would take up all of Main Street, which was pretty much the only street in and out of the village, and the farmers' carriages and the occasional car would have to wait until it passed through. Guests would hardly get off in the small village which had nothing to offer for city folks. With two bakeries, a butcher shop and a handful of "rustic" restaurants frequented by the locals, there simply was not much to explore. The only department store did not deserve the name, according to Henry, as it was a narrow, dark shop stretching over just one floor. Compare that to this neighborhood, she thought.

He surely would miss getting the "Staats", his beloved newspaper, from the paper boy around the corner and picking up his favorite cigars at McKinney's tobacco shop, just as she would miss her parents' Delicatessen or the window displays in the more fashionable stores she enjoyed so much on their strolls to the park.

She wondered how Henry would be able to support their family in the old village. After all, how many suits would a villager own in his lifetime? One for work, one to go to church and get married in, and if he did not gain too much weight, to get buried in as well. There had been no place for a second tailor in the village, and Henry's own father had not been ready to leave the business to his son back then. The vineyards the family had owned for generations had been sold over the decades, his father showed no interest in wine-making, and the few remaining were farmed by their neighbors in exchange for 100 bottles of wine annually. 100 bottles! Those were gone quickly, she was sure of it. The old barn on the open side of the three-winged farmhouse had been sold off, and a brick wall separated the lots now. The stable in the side wing had long been empty, and so were the two deep wine cellars – except for those 100 bottles with the limited shelf life. Henry's three sisters had received a nice dowry after the sales, and he had held on to his share which turned out to be enough to get him started here. With too much time on his hands for lack of customers and a strict father whom he could never please, Heinrich, as he had been called then, had dreamed of another future in a different place.

That fight: a simple shouting match, a bit of wrestling perhaps, had he really knocked out that fellow? One crate was already full. She would have to leave the red velvet curtains behind, they simply were too bulky. She really liked how they made the living room look comfortable, or did until she took them down this morning. Maybe Mama would want them to replace her bedroom curtains or use the fabric for a dress. Reluctantly, Elizabeth put the long shawls on a chair.

After the wedding, Mama and Papa had helped them move Henry's shop to a better location with a good-sized apartment on the second floor, large enough for a young family. That was when they had given her that special wedding gift: a large framed picture of an elegant couple on their wedding night. They were embracing passionately, but fully clothed, of course, in front of a stately poster bed. White curtains blowing gently in a summer breeze added a dreamlike atmosphere, the husband in his dark wedding suit gently held her in his arms, their lips almost touching. The dark-haired bride looked shy and pure in her gauzy white dress, yet ready to return his kiss, enjoy sexual bliss and a life of fulfillment with the love of her life. This was the life she had imagined for herself and Henry when she had placed that picture over her own wedding bed. What a happy couple. It was probably just a common print fashionable at the time, she could not tell. But the light brown frame of carved rose vines embroidered with little pieces of mother of pearl gave it a stately look.

Life had been good, for a while. Henry's business allowed for small luxuries like Sunday dinners in a restaurant after their customary walk in the park to parade their modest wealth. And when she had been expecting, her happiness could not have been greater. Lilly had been born in January, and Mama and Papa had given her a matching picture with the same light brown carved frame she had hung over her bed: the same couple, with the young wife dressed in black, as any respectable woman would, but with a bit more weight on her delicate frame, and a baby in her arms, a little doll whose face was peeking out of an abundance of lace and frills. She still could not tell if it was a boy or a girl. The husband, stately, mature, yet affectionately looking at his little family, was placed in the middle of his elegantly furnished living room, which looked a bit dark because of the wooden paneling and the dark-brown cupboards. Everything appeared as it should be: solid, secure, respectable, and with a quiet dignity.

Elizabeth remembered pulling out the nail which had centered the picture over the bed and moved it further to the left to make room for its twin. She had tried to have them both at exactly the same level, but since she never had the patience to measure before hanging anything on the wall, there had been a slight difference. Henry had noticed it, of course, and kept complaining about it. But he never pulled that nail, or picked up that hammer, to make it right.

Starting to fill the second overseas crate, she paused to look at these framed versions of married life leaning against the sofa. There was the couple frozen in perpetual passion-to-come on their wedding night; and here they were, proud parents to a little bundle of joy, probably nine months later, because in a story, even if it's framed, everything is meant to be perfect. A framed life in two still pictures. How did their story continue?

Lilly had not survived her first birthday, and there was nothing she could have done to prevent it. Lilly's heart had not been strong enough, beating too fast like a little bird's, and her own had almost broken. She had become pregnant again, and again, seven times over the years, seven miscarriages, and nobody knew why. Every time she had been so full of hope and *Sehnsucht* to hold that little being in her arms and never let it go.

But Lilly had been the only baby she ever held, and with each failed pregnancy her world became smaller, darker. They had almost given up hope, when number nine, the final one, was born – and meant to live.

Little Henry, a miniature version of his father with bright blue eyes and golden hair, was a timid, sensitive child. She worried about him a lot, worried he could harm himself, fall, be run over by a carriage or catch this dreadful fever that had killed some of the children in the neighborhood. She doted on him, and whenever Henry talked about turning him into a "real boy", she protected Little Henry. He had become the center of attention, the love of her life. How much she enjoyed dressing him up in beautiful costumes, turning him into a little man wearing a fine dark-brown suit or a little blue military jacket with brass buttons and a high waist, a Russian hat and warm coat for harsh Manhattan winter days. She had his picture taken, the ones she was about to slide between one of her scarves in crate number one, over and over again in Henry Schoerry's Studio down on the corner of Avenue A and Third Street.

Here he was, Little Henry looking proudly and seriously into the camera performing for his mother and trying to hold that position a minute or more for the bulky camera to take that perfect picture. The cardboard photographs had decorated the house and the shop, where they served as advertisement for children's outfits with Little Henry as the model child. Big Henry had sent them to his folks in the old country, his son, Little Henry, so well dressed and good looking, just like his father. After the photo shoot, Elizabeth often rewarded the boy's patience with a walk to Grand Central Station, which was not far away, to watch the trains come in or leave. At times like that, she remembered her childhood dreams about travels to far-away places and would share them with Little Henry.

Baby Henry

Life *was* good, for the most part, with Little Henry being the joyous center of their lives. But there were dark days as well. The pregnancies had taken much of her strength and energy away, she sometimes felt sad because she blamed herself for not giving Big Henry the children he wanted and for not having been able to keep Lilly alive. Why did they never talk about it? At first their grief had been too strong, made them numb. But with each failed pregnancy she could feel their relationship changing, become distanced. They were polite, maneuvered everyday life like a well-functioning couple. And yet, as much as he tried, Henry just could not

Little Henry — Model Child

make her laugh again. When he came home at night and wanted to tell her about his day, what his pompous, well-off customer had demanded of him, she often turned away without even noticing it. Had she perhaps neglected

Henry? Did he feel excluded from the close relationship, the deep love she shared with Little Henry?

Elizabeth wrapped two brown woolen blankets around each heavy picture frame covering the sensual couple and protecting the joyous family. She placed them on the bottom of crate number two. Perhaps she could wrap them in her velvet curtains instead, she wondered. But, no, she would certainly need blankets in the drafty old place she would live in. The curtains would have to stay behind.

She suspected Henry had his own way of dealing with the tragedies in their life. Hiding the pain deep in his heart, he was taking his time coming home after closing shop for the night. He often stopped in the beer bars, drank with men from the old country who told each other stories of their youth and their dreams of a grand future. A future that would never happen, she was sure about that.

Sometimes Henry lost his temper, could be impatient with folks around him. When Martin, the fourteen-year-old boy working in the shop learning to become a tailor himself, did not thread that needle fast enough or dropped the scissors, Henry would throw anything in his reach, sometimes the needle box. The boy then had to pick them up, one by one, scattered between the pieces of fabric on the floor. Henry was particular, took good care of his tools, kept the scissors sharp and embroidered with great patience the button holes and cuffs of a new coat. Often, when she came down to the shop to bring him lunch, Elizabeth would find Henry lost in his work. She detected a melancholy in his eyes, and felt her heart contracting. She remembered how much she had been in love with him back then on the park bench in Tompkins Square Park, and part of her still was. *Sehnsucht* in his eyes, a deep longing, for what she wasn't sure, somehow did not include her. What was he thinking about sitting cross-legged on the table, embroidering that fancy velvet vest? Maybe about his old home with its peaceful, ordered landscape of rows and rows of vines climbing the hills that he had described to her over and over again? Things had changed with all the dead children between them. Sorrow had crept into their home and heart and kept them from talking. They both focused on Little Henry instead, the subject of their love and care.

And then there were those letters from home urging Henry to come and visit. Henry and his father had never been close, but his mother missed her only son. How would she feel if Little Henry lived so far away from her? And how would her parents feel if she did not live around the corner, but across an ocean. They were getting older. Would Clara be able to take care of them? Henry's mother wanted to see him one more time reminding her son that he had been talking for years about visiting the old home, taking Elizabeth and Little Henry to meet his folks. And when Henry was invited to a cousin's wedding, he finally decided to go, almost 20 years after he had run off, alone. Henry was to travel by boat from New York to Bremerhaven, and from there by train to his home region on the Rhine river. He planned to be gone for a month or two and gave instructions to John on how to run the shop properly, as if he did not know, and to look after Elizabeth and Little Henry. He did not want them to come along, shunned the expenses for all three of them. Elizabeth wondered if he also felt he had to go on this trip alone to find out where he belonged. She had packed his light linen summer suit, a couple shirts with replaceable collars and his silk handkerchiefs. Henry put on a traveling suit made of light grey wool with a matching hat. He was ready to impress.

Henry's letters arrived irregularly, but they were surprisingly long and detailed. He wrote about his long trip to the old country and how excited people were to see him again. There was a tone that alarmed her. What he had not been able to say, he now wrote about, it seemed.

Henry wrote that the old friends found him changed, bigger and more mature, but soon they reconnected telling each other stories about past school days. They wanted to know all about the busy life in the big city, the many attractions and if life was easier there. Henry probably exaggerated his income just a little bit, but she knew he looked so fine in his grey woolen suit and silk hat that they believed anything he said. He had always been a gifted storyteller. Each evening, he wrote, he would go to Else's little wine place on his street to find laughter and comradery. Why had he ever left, he wondered? Sure, the village was still a small place with now three bakeries, two butcher shops and that same dark department store where people could buy anything from pots to underwear. Main Street looked even more narrow with the train tracks now laid, and everything seemed smaller than he remembered. But then he would walk out into the countryside, look from the hills down to the old river, sit by the Rhine watching the barks go all the way to the North Sea. He loved the geometrical design of the vineyards, row after row giving structure to the landscape.

Henry confessed that he worried about his New York business, about having fewer customers. He and John had not really talked much about it, but both noticed it. Big factories with hundreds of seamstresses, mostly recently arrived immigrant women who made pitiful wages, had opened up north. Cheap clothing started to flood the department stores in the city. He only knew how to sew. What would he do if business got worse? Before too long, he wouldn't be able to pay John and the boy their wages. Could he keep the business open on his own? He was known as a very meticulous tailor who only worked with fine fabrics. But his customers, the ones he had served for many years, were getting older. Would the younger folks still need a tailor, or would they go to the big department stores on Fifth Avenue? They wouldn't have to wait for their suits and coats to be ready. In his letter, Henry told her that before he left, he had actually gone to one of those stores to look at the rows of suits displayed in the showrooms. Sure, they weren't tailored to the customer's needs and body. The button holes had not been carefully and accurately embroidered by hand but quickly, with a sewing machine so that a few loose threads were showing. But the department stores offered to alter suits right there if they didn't fit properly and for a good price. They even guaranteed to do it within a day and deliver the suit to the doorstep! Customers could choose among sizes and colors and take their new piece home right away.

What if he decided to stay in the village, in the old country, she worried. Nobody in his village had ever left, well, maybe a few, but most were never heard of again. The farm boys had married a girl from their own or a neighboring village, worked in the vineyards and fields from spring to fall, and in the cellars in the winter. They never went anywhere. Henry told them stories about the big city, the cars replacing the horse drawn carriages, the immigrants from all over the world, the German and Italian neighborhoods and his rich customers. Maybe the tourists taking the small train to the fashionable spa three miles north of his home village would find the successful tailor from New York an attraction, get off that train, visit his shop in the old farmhouse or ask him to take their measurements in their fancy hotels and place an order with him?

How much did she still mean to him? Elizabeth pushed that thought aside. Who in his right mind would go back to this backward place, this village that never changed, where everybody knew each other and nobody ever forgot anything? Wasn't that one of the reasons why Mama and Papa had left their home town? Because her Catholic father had married a Protestant girl, and even though Mama converted, neither of the two congregations in their town approved of it.

Henry had been away for almost two months now, but she really did not mind that much. Actually, she enjoyed that little bit of extra freedom, time to spend with her parents and with Little Henry. Lunch did not have to be on the table or taken down to the shop by noon, and nobody told her how to run her household or raise her child. She wasn't worried about Henry staying out too late after work, drinking too much and spending his hard-earned money in the pub.

She put down the underwear she had been folding. When did this start? When did he stop being that charming, witty fellow, always ready to tell a funny story, adding a bit here and there to make her laugh? When did he turn into that quiet, brooding person, never touching her any more, not even kissing her when he left for work or came home? Only when he played with Little Henry or took him out for a Sunday walk did his dimpled smile appear and light up his face. He never looked at her with that warm expression any more. What had gone wrong?

She noticed that even Little Henry acted as if some weight had been lifted off his small shoulders. As much as he loved his father, he always felt like he had to perform for him, make him happy, impress him with … something. She knew that Little Henry made up stories about being the fastest during the sports classes in the

Turnverein or scoring a winning goal during a soccer match. Little Henry hated his sports lessons. He was neither the fastest nor the strongest kid. Nobody wanted him on his team when they played soccer. But she never told on him. Alone with her, she let him draw and daydream as much as he liked. Though enrolled in elementary school, Henry, a frail child, often stayed with her, and she enjoyed having him close. Now he had plenty of time to sit by the bay window and watch the busy East Village street, go to the market with her and watch the coaches and cars go by. Maybe he would go to art school some day and become a teacher.

John, finally in charge, would check on them every day, flirting a little with Elizabeth in his good-natured way. He had a wife and six kids to feed, no danger there. John always complimented Little Henry on his drawings. She felt that he, too, was relieved that his boss was not around to correct his stitches and criticize his work. Though they had started the business together, Henry had always made sure that John knew he was number two. Henry worked only for the best customers who ordered several suits and shirts per year. John could deal with the ones who had to save their money to pay for one good suit, perhaps for their wedding. You would leave several inches in the seams to let out so they could come back years later to have that suit altered when they got heavier with age. John was the one to work with these smelly old clothes that were only brushed off, seldom washed.

That summer, life had a tranquility she had never experienced before. But this blissful time was not to last. A short letter arrived turning her life upside down:

Dear Lisa (he had not called her that in years, preferred "mother" instead),

I have come to a decision. I want you to sell everything we own. I'm sure, John will buy the shop. He has long wanted to be a full partner, anyway. I'm not coming back. Sell everything and take the boat with Henry to join me here. I know this will be difficult for you, leaving the world you know and your parents behind. And should you decide to stay in Manhattan, I understand. But please know that I will never give up my only son.

She, of course, obeyed. How could she not? Legally, she had no rights to her child when the father demanded him. Giving up the one person she loved so deeply and sending him to live in a country he did not know, without a mother?

Though Papa wept when she showed him the letter, he told her a wife had to stay with her husband, go wherever he wants her to go. Her religion told her the same. Even if she took Little Henry and tried a life on her own, she had no money, no skills, and her parents, even if they wanted to, were not able to support them both. They had hired Alfred, a cousin, to help out in the store who had suffered from polio as a boy and nobody else would give him a job. Even if she wanted to work in the Deli, she would push him out because Papa could not pay for both of them. Clara might be able to help, Elizabeth thought. They had not seen each other in more than a year, and then only briefly when she visited for Christmas. Clara had always been suspicious of Henry, never cared much for him and thought it a mistake to get married at such an early age.

Elizabeth decided to swallow her pride and write a letter to Clara who was performing in Boston for a few weeks. Anxiously she was waiting for her reply which arrived within a week:

Dear Elizabeth,

I so much would like to help you. Yes, I'm making my own money, but though we are concert artists, we don't make half as much as our male colleagues. It might sound glamorous that we play in the most distinguished concert halls. But we often perform in beer halls and restaurants as well to be able to make a living. But I do what I love most, playing the violin, and it does give me a certain independence. I'm saving for old age because I don't suspect that any dashing fellow will come along and take care of me. Even if this happened, I probably would have to give up my current life, which I simply couldn't. No, this isn't meant to criticize you, but I'm afraid you made your choice. I'm sorry that you will live so far away, but I promise to look after Mama and Papa. I'm hoping to travel to Europe with our orchestra, and if I do, I will visit you. Please write often and take good care of Little Henry. This won't be easy for him either, but at least he has you–and his father. Life takes funny turns, so don't give up hope.

Your loving sister Clara

She could not take much, not the furniture, nor the pretty cups and plates or her red velvet curtains. She had finished wrapping everything up, Henry's set of scissors that he insisted she should bring, the cardboard photographs taken in Henry Schoerry's Studio, the two large pictures now wrapped in brown woolen blankets to protect the carved frames and glass that Mama and Papa had given her. The first, after the wedding, the second after her little baby girl Lilly was born.

She closed the second crate. She had wrapped up her dreams, of a happy marriage, good schools and maybe even art school for Little Henry, and a comfortable life in this big, exciting city near her parents. The next day she and Little Henry would go on that trip crossing the vast ocean. Not to pursue adventures she had dreamed about as a girl, but to travel to a home and a country that weren't hers or her son's.

She never forgave Henry.

* * * * *

EPILOGUE

The wood-framed pictures are all that remain of Elizabeth, and a few photographs, handed down to the following generations. One of them is a group photo taken on the Pennsylvania sailing back to the old country. It shows a woman in a white blouse and skirt with an abundance of dark hair and a little leather purse strung across her chest. She is standing close to her boy, the best dressed little fellow of the group. Both look straight into the camera, a bit too serious, perhaps, but people did not smile in photographs back then.

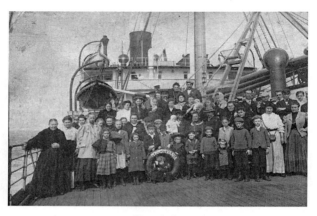

"Returning"

The train tracks through the village were torn out in the 1930s. Tourist numbers had long dropped by then, and space was needed for cars. Elizabeth did not live to see Little Henry get married and have kids of his own, a boy and a girl. Else, the owner of the little wine pub on their street where Big Henry and Little Henry, who continued the family tradition, would go after work, recalled Elizabeth many, many years later. She was "the sad woman from New York, Heinrich's wife, who did not even own a winter coat, just a woolen shawl although her husband was a tailor." She would not part with her son who would always be called Henry, the

Ami, in that small village not far away from the banks of the Rhine.

When Life Was Good —Elizabeth

THREE
Little Henry
1907-1917

He knew that his German sounded funny, had a Swabian melody to it, his grandparents' and mother's dialect, with his sentences ending on a question mark. He could hear it. And his "r" had that round, American quality. This was not how people spoke here, and the boys who asked him to come and play soccer on the dirt patch in front of the school were puzzled. They were curious about the Ami. Sometimes they did not understand what he said, and, although his father spoke the local dialect, Little Henry had trouble following the quick speaking patterns of the boys. They called him "Hennrrii" not Heinrich or Heini, as some others in the village were called. He was "Hennrrii" which sounded like they lingered on the *n*, pushed on the *r* and drew out the *i*. The softness in "Henry" was gone. But there was a certain excitement in how they pronounced his name, an expectation, a call to join them.

The Atlantic crossing and the train ride had been long, yet exciting. It had felt a little bit like an adventure, like travels Jules Verne would have described in a book featuring Little Henry as the main character. Of course, no such book existed, but only because he and Jules

Verne had never met. Little Henry loved adventure books with heroes who would travel the globe in eighty days to break a record, discover the middle of the earth, search for sea monsters in the deep sea, win the heart of a beautiful woman and return in triumph to one's home town. His mother had read to him during the trip, though she had fought travel sickness on the boat, and Little Henry's imagination had soared. He had loved watching the men working the boat, the waves changing color, depending on how blue or grey the sky was. He could not stop staring at the vast net of stars in some of the clear nights. But when the seas had turned rough, he had been glad not to be alone and had snuggled up to his mother, although he was almost too old for that. At least that's what his father would have said: "When I was your age . . .", and Little Henry's thoughts automatically began to wander.

Although Little Henry had known that all their belongings and his father's shop had been sold with the exception of whatever fitted into two oversea crates, he had felt like he was only going on a vacation. He had pushed away the troubling thoughts: that he was leaving behind friends, his grandparents, Aunt Clara and John, the tailor. Only slowly had it sunk in that he was meant to stay and live with these old people in the farmhouse in the center of a small village.

It had taken him only an afternoon to explore the place. There was a little bakery across the narrow main street, a butcher's next to their house, the church up the road and the school five minutes down the street across the small market place, three if he ran. This was a plus, short distances, when he overslept or day dreamed in the morning under the blanket that was so warm and cozy, and the house was not. Also, right outside his room was a steep ladder leading up to the open attic which looked dark and scared him. He tried not to look up when he walked by, but no matter how hard he tried, his head almost turned automatically and his eyes fixed on the dark square in the ceiling. His mother had to come to his room three, four times to get him up, would finally grab him by his hand, which was exactly what he wanted, and dragged him down the stairs to the warm kitchen while picking up his scattered clothes from the floor where he had left them the night before. There was no time for breakfast then, but Mama would have prepared a buttered sandwich with sugar sprinkled on top of it to eat on the way out or during the first break. No time to wash or brush teeth. The other boys also looked like they never washed, just jumped into their trousers and sweaters that had silver traces on the sleeves. Hankies were for losers.

Everybody was curious about the newcomers, a little suspicious perhaps because they had lived abroad in that big foreign city. But Big Henry, or Heinrich, as they had always called him and which he now became again, was one of them. So his wife and his son belonged as well. After all, they had come back to stay, which meant they really wanted to be here. So, village life wasn't so bad after all, they thought. The family "chose" to come back, folks said, because Heinrich had been homesick. Only now Little Henry was homesick. The roles had reversed.

In his narrow bed with the tall head- and footboard, the other half of what used to be his great grandparents' wedding bed, Little Henry dreamed of his old home. He conjured up the view from the bay window, his favorite spot where he used to sit and draw. Street noise was floating up, vendors calling out their goods, newspaper boys announcing sports results in their high voices, horse-drawn coal carts going by and automobiles pushing them out of the way. His mother was busy in the kitchen preparing lunch or dinner and singing to herself. At least that was what she used to do. Here, in her mother-in-law's kitchen, she didn't sing. She'd be banging pots and pans which weren't her own, trying to scrape off the blackened grease. Little Henry's thoughts returned to the present. Sometimes she was crying silently. He did not know how to help her. For a while his parents had argued a lot, accusing the other of ruining each other's lives. After a while that stopped. They would not even speak. They simply existed next to each other.

Little Henry knew that he needed to become part of village life. He knew that he needed to belong, and the first step was to speak like the other boys. He had an ear for language, after all he had been living in a two-language family because his New York based grandparents had still spoken German with each other. English was of no use whatsoever in this new environment, so he needed to focus; he needed to learn the dialect. *Hessisch*. It wasn't as difficult as he thought. Henry started to pick up little expressions that made how he talked sound authentic. For no real reason people often started a sentence with "Ei", which did not mean "Ei," the German word for "egg". Actually, it meant nothing. It was just the way they started a sentence, like "Also", or "Well" in English. That's how he started: "Ei, guude," people would say to each other, a short form of "good day" or "guten Tag." Or "Ei guude, wie?" as in "Hello, how are you," just shorter. Henry started to pick up the melody of the dialect and the economizing. People saved on words, unless they gossiped. Henry had not reached that master level yet, but he would get there. Surely people were gossiping about him and his mother, not just because they had moved here, weren't born here, which was a clear disadvantage in their eyes. Also because his mother kept to herself, didn't talk much, wasn't seeking friendships. She was unhappy. Clearly so.

Little Henry didn't want to be seen as an unhappy boy, so he joined the boys who called him "Hennrriii" in the school yard. But he was not a sportsman, he knew that only too well. At all costs, Henry was trying to avoid the reputation he had had at his Manhattan school: the boy who sucked at sports, who was mama's boy, a wimp. And so Henry concentrated on what he was good at. He had a great imagination, and he was a good storyteller. Henry reinvented himself. He discovered that he could be sly, that he could stretch the truth, and nobody would ever know–except his parents. But since his mother kept to herself and his father wasn't interested in gossip, they might never find out.

"I wish I could play soccer with you," Little Henry would say, "but I'm strictly forbidden to play sports. I might lose my ability to walk, end up in a wheel chair." The boys would stare at him, which encouraged Little Henry to go on: "Don't you know" or "Ei, wisst er dann nit …" (he had practiced that), "Don't you know that I used to play ice hockey in the little league in New York?" He made this up completely, but remembered watching the older boys play hockey on the frozen lake in the park. Never would he have even stepped onto the icy surface for fear of breaking through. Death by drowning, and that in icy, black water, the thought alone had caused him nightmares. And his mother wouldn't have let him anyway, let alone that a hockey little league didn't exist.

"My father gave me ice skates for Christmas when I was five year's old, and the carpenter in our street carved me a wooden stick. The best stick tailored to my body and my swing. We practiced every Saturday and played teams from all over the city on Sundays." The boys wanted to know more, so he made up stories about the games they won, the goals he scored, up to that horrible accident when he fell hard because some bully had tackled him, broke through the ice with a half-cracked spine and was rescued at the last minute, no, the last second, by a dog who had dragged him out by his sleeve. The dog and Little Henry had become great friends, but he had to leave him behind. Since then he could not play ice hockey any more, nor soccer, or run, which was really too bad because he had been one of the best players. This was the moment when he would start crying, just a little bit, then visibly pull himself together like a man to say: "But I can cheer you on and give you advice on how to play better. It's all strategy anyway, in hockey or in soccer." The boys were impressed, wiped their noses on their sleeves because they, too, had become emotional and slapped Henry on his back, carefully. "Ei, gut", they would say, and resume their game, occasionally waving at Henry who acted like he had become their coach. They were happy because they had never had a coach, and Henry was an Ami who simply knew more about sports, didn't he?

When the school master asked his mother if Little Henry really could not participate in school sports because of an injury to his back, Elizabeth hesitated, thought for a moment and then said: "Yes, it's true, unfortunately, because Henry loves sports. I asked our family doctor in New York to send me a letter describing the injury, but it hasn't arrived yet." She was buying time for Little Henry. She knew how difficult it was for him to adapt to his new home. The school master seemed satisfied, asked once or twice for the letter, but since it never came, he decided to forget about it and simply marked in the school certificate that Henry was excused from participating in school sports. "Why go through all that trouble finding out if it's true or not," he thought when filling out the certificates at the end of the term. He had enough on his hands with these stupid village boys and girls who weren't really interested in learning anyway. Future farmers, factory workers and housewives, that would be their life. No ambition here, not even that small boy from New York showed much promise.

The school master had been running this tiny school for almost 30 years now. Two classrooms for grades one to four, and five to eight. Religion and music were taught for the whole group with the older students making fun of the younger ones. The gymnasium, if you could call it that, was a dusty place under the roof with equipment the children's fathers and mothers had already used: large leather balls too heavy to lift for the children and ropes to climb, which most of them hated because the ropes were old, not smooth and would scrape your hands. With their thin arms they made it half way up and kept dangling there afraid to fall. Then there was the balance beam the boys hated because balancing made them look like sissies, and a wooden ladder against the wall to climb up and down as quickly as possible with their teacher, sports, math, German and science teacher all in one, stopping the time. He hated it as much as the children and was glad when they could go outside where he read while the boys were playing soccer and the girls tag. Once in a while the soccer ball landed in the little creek which ran along the school yard, and one of the boys got his feet wet when fishing the ball out of the water. He had to be quick because the current swiftly carried the ball down towards the river. Everybody got excited then, the girls interrupting their play to watch, hoping the boy would slip and get all wet. But a few minutes later when the ball rescuer triumphantly climbed out of the water, the match continued and the teacher turned once again to his book. Another normal, boring school day.

Henry didn't mind school. It got him out of the house, and the boys accepted him. He wasn't so bad at math, and he loved his art lessons although he did not really learn much. At least he was allowed to do what he wanted, so he drew the *Pennsylvania*, the boat that had carried him and his mother to Hamburg, the waves in their different shades, the busy streets of Manhattan and automobiles which he loved. His mother pinned the drawings to the wall with needles that left traces in the old wallpaper when you moved them to make room for new ones. The plaster behind the wallpaper sometimes crumbled and sailed down the wall. Henry was curious about what was hiding behind the old-fashioned pink flowers and faded green leaves and scraped away the old paper behind his bed. Behind the plaster he found straw packed into clay which filled the space between the beams. At night he could hear mice moving in the tunnels they had eaten into the plaster. When he discovered a tiny round exit in the corner of his room, he placed breadcrumbs in front of it hoping he would catch sight of the rodent family that shared his home. He regularly fell asleep while waiting for them to peek out of that hole, and in the morning the breadcrumbs were gone.

Life was fairly uneventful, except when Heinrich took him along on short trips to his customers in the spa town not far away. Both would get on their bikes with a little cart attached to his father's which carried the carefully wrapped suits and coats. The boy tried hard to keep up with his father's swift pace, but the black bike was too big for him, and he could not sit and pedal at the same time. It was worth it, though, because while his father was fitting the customer, Little Henry sat waiting for him in the hotel lobby watching the fashionable guests get ready for a walk, to take the waters or attend the daily concert. When his customers tipped him well, which greatly improved Heinrich's mood, he sometimes bought the boy a hot chocolate and a large piece of golden cheesecake. Then it felt a little bit like their Sunday walks in the park back in America.

Little Henry finished school at age 14, still a small boy who looked more like twelve. To make up for that he started smoking, only when he was with the boys, of course, stealing cigars from his father, biting off the tip, spitting it out and lighting the cigar with a match, slowly puffing like he had seen his father do it. He loved the wooden cigar boxes and the banderoles around the cigar which he collected. They told stories about foreign lands and peoples, and he wondered where the tobacco had been harvested, dried, who had rolled that cigar and packed it together with its brothers into small, wooden boxes that smelled of tobacco and far-away places. He dreamed about traveling.

Yet, Little Henry did what was expected of him, at least for a while: an apprenticeship with his father to become a master tailor in the fifth generation or so. Not that he loved the profession, but he had no idea what else to do. He had watched his father for years and knew his role: first of all, keep the floor clean so discarded cloth and thread would not catch fire or dirty the expensive suits; oil the Singer, but carefully as not to soil the fabric; exchange the broken needle if needed; learn how to take measurements, make a pattern out of newspapers, and prepare the pieces for sewing; eventually be allowed to cut the fabric after pinning the paper pattern onto it without tipping over the box of needles set on the edge of the table. And then, eventually, after years of being scolded, corrected and often yelled at because he just, according to his perfectionist father, could not do the chores, he would be allowed to make a whole suit.

But it never came to that. Almost three years into his apprenticeship Little Henry finally could not take his father's frequent rages anymore, his impatience with a not-so-talented son whose goal seemed to be to not be seen or heard, who much rather sat in the kitchen with his mother than do what he was supposed to do. After a particularly violent verbal abuse, Little Henry finally threw the shirt he was working on in front of his father's feet, ripped the newspaper pattern into four pieces, threw them in the air and shouted: "Ei loss misch doch in Ruh! Mach Deinen Scheiß allons!" (leave me alone, do your own shit). Little Henry was trembling, but he felt strangely excited. He walked out the door, dragged his bike out of the shed and took off.

At least this was the version he told his friends, that he had had the courage to walk out on his father, to quit. What really happened was this: Heinrich was in a particularly irritable mood. His wife kept coughing during breakfast, his mother complained endlessly about the cold spring while his son kept looking out the window daydreaming, as usual, instead of finishing the shirt that was to be delivered the next day together with a full suit and vest. Twice did he have to remove the collar which Little Henry had stitched on rather sloppily, the fabric already showing traces of smudge and wear. Heinrich could not afford to hire skilled help like John, whom he missed terribly, and this thought made him even more irritable because it would lead to the next, which was questioning his decision to return to Germany; and the next, questioning his marriage, his son's abilities, his whole, boring, stupid life in this godforsaken village. And when Little Henry showed up late in the shop with traces of butter on his shirt, his father kicked him out, shouting that he would never amount to anything, let alone becoming a good tailor like himself.

So the only correct version of Little Henry's story which he later told his friends was that he was out of a job, would not finish the apprenticeship, and that he would be the first Henry in generations not to spend his life bent over a piece of fabric and a sewing machine. He would be . . . what would he be?, Henry thought while letting his bike roll downhill towards the river. Things would be o.k. He could start working in the factory half way between the village and the spa town. They always needed workers. He could save money and buy a ticket back to New York. He would be free to do whatever he wanted. He just needed time to find out what that was. He sat by the banks of the river for the rest of the day, watching the Rhine barks go by, dreading to go home. What if he just tried to get on one of the boats, just like his father had done when he was only a little older than himself? If he managed to make it all the way to New York, maybe he could stay with his Aunt Clara, work in his grandparents' Deli which a cousin now owned?

But then he thought of his mother whom he could not part from. He finally got up, because it got dark and the air chilly, wiped the grass off his damp bottom and decided to put off his plans for now. He picked up the black old bike which was still too big for him and worked his way up the hill. There was a light still on in his father's shop, but Henry quietly snuck into his own room. Dropping his pants and shirt in front of the bed, he crawled under the blanket leaving his socks on because his feet were still cold. In the morning he would apply for a job in the factory. He had his own pride, Little Henry, and he wouldn't beg his father to take him back. Not yet, at least.

FOUR
Clara
1917

The brown, water-stained envelope had been forwarded from the old address, her parents' place, where she hadn't lived for a year. She had been forced to give it up after they had died, too big, too expensive. That, and because the letter had come from overseas, had caused a four-week delay, at least. She looked at the large left leaning letters written in black ink—as if the person who had copied the address onto the envelope was not used to writing a lot.

"Miss Clara Schombart" it said. It was not her sister's handwriting.

She opened the envelope with a small sharp kitchen knife that she used to peel potatoes when she actually had time to cook. "Küchen-Peter," her mother had called it. "Kitchen-Peter," what a funny term for a simple knife. "Wo ist mein Küchen-Peter," she would shout when she could not find it in the drawer or the kitchen sink, suspecting she had thrown out the precious utensil with the potato peels, those long spiral strips she carefully produced and then wrapped in newspaper to put into the trash. She had always found the knife when she looked in the drawer or the sink a second time. It had been her best among kitchen knives of all lengths, and it would not be easy to replace. Now Clara owned it, one of the few items she had taken from her parents' household after they had died within weeks from each other. Some couples did, their hearts simply broken, and the void the loved one left could not be filled ever again. "One's other half", some people called it, you simply couldn't live without it.

Clara enjoyed a home-cooked meal when she returned from a concert tour. Then she would cook her mother's recipes, potato salad, wieners, sauerbraten with raisins and dumplings. Klöße, Mama had called them. And sweet dishes like pancakes with plum sauce. She often invited her best friend Ruth, also a musician in the orchestra and also without a family. She didn't live far away, just a few blocks from her apartment on Thompson Street. So walking back home in the dark after dinner wasn't a problem. Not that Ruth or Clara would have been afraid to maneuver the city on their own. They knew their closed-knit neighborhood.

It was a short letter, barely a page, written in English with a few German expressions mixed in, as if the writer had struggled to remember some of the words. Her hands began to tremble in anticipation of what was to come.

"Liebe Clara", it said, *"I know this will make you sad, but I must tell you that Elizabeth, Deine Schwester, died a few days ago. Verstorben. She caught a cold and ran a high fever for days. I think she died of a Lungenentzündung, I forgot what the word is in English. It happened so fast, I never expected this. Little Henry is sehr traurig, very sad, as you can imagine. He keeps mainly to himself, and I don't know what to say to him. Wir sprechen nicht so oft miteinander. I know that Elizabeth wasn't happy here. I tried to help her, introduced her to neighbors and friends, but fact is she never wanted to come. Was it the right decision to bring the family back to the village? I have asked myself the question many times, immer und immer wieder. Elizabeth and I never talked about it, couldn't talk about it without me shouting at her, and Elizabeth looking at me with her beautiful, sad eyes. Well, it's too late now. Lisa is gone."*

The letter concluded with a quote: "*Schiffe ruhig weiter, wenn der Mast auch bricht . . .*" (sail on even when your mast has broken) and it was signed by Big Henry, her brother-in-law.

She remembered that quote from her father, a religious man, it was one of his favorites. But Henry had left out the part about God: "*Gott ist Dein Begleiter, er vergisst Dich nicht*" (God is your companion, he does not forget you). He sure wouldn't have discovered God, not even after his wife's death. That wasn't him. But he did sound sorry, sad even, although Clara knew that the marriage had been rocky even before he had forced her sister to leave Manhattan. Elizabeth had fallen silent, gone mute. The only person she had talked to was Little Henry, and Clara through occasional letters.

Clara sat down by the kitchen table, the letter still in her hand. She was the older sister by three years, turning fifty in a few months. This was not an age to die, these weren't the Middle Ages, there should be decades ahead of them, at least two. Time for travels, concerts, and for Elizabeth to see her son getting married, having grandchildren. Her sister in that old drafty farmhouse, no wonder she fell ill, caught a cold. *Lungenentzündung* – something with the lungs. Henry probably had not taken it seriously enough, had not wanted to spend the money on a doctor. He was a penny pincher, always had been one. Elizabeth had to ask him for a few coins just to buy stamps, while he spent the money in that dingy pub every evening after dinner, seeking the company of drinking men and the pub owner, a local woman he had gone to school with. He had left Elizabeth and Little Henry to themselves avoiding any kind of conversation. He could not face his wife who had turned into a living accusation.

Henry had not always been like that. Clara also remembered him as a witty fellow, polite and warm. That was when he had first been calling on Elizabeth. He had often teased Clara in a good-natured way about her constant practicing. Sometimes the three of them would go for a walk. Or they would sing together with Clara and her father accompanying them on their violins. Henry had a nice, warm baritone and could hold his tune.

Clara checked the dates again. The funeral had probably taken place at least three weeks ago. She had been playing in Buffalo then. She could not have attended anyway, not with the busy fall schedule the orchestra kept and the trip crossing the Atlantic by boat taking forever. And there was the war going on. German U-boats had been torpedoing passenger ships, the papers were full of it, and American troops were being mustered to be shipped overseas. It was not a good time to travel, or to be seen as an American of German descent. Going on a trip to Germany, even for the purpose of attending her sister's funeral, to some would have looked like she was still loyal to that country. She wasn't. Except for Little Henry, nothing tied her to the old country now. She was an American woman and supporting herself. A modern, independent woman.

It would have been difficult if not impossible to get to the village. Nor would she have wanted to see the place that had made her sister so unhappy. Why would anyone want to go back? Didn't they all come to America, the "huddled masses," to start anew and leave the old world behind? She had been too young to understand this at the time her family had arrived, but it was what her father had been saying over and over again: "The best decision in my life," he would say, although he, too, had to make sacrifices.

It would be nice to see Little Henry again, Clara thought. He had just turned nineteen. She loved the little fellow, and childless herself, she had been heartbroken when he and Elizabeth had followed Big Henry to the old country. Clara and her parents never would have thought that this was to be a good-bye forever. At the time Clara had hoped to visit Elizabeth and dreamed about combining the trip with taking a few master classes in Stuttgart or Leipzig, maybe even Berlin, the centers of musical excellence. Any musician who aspired high had been doing this for decades, go to France or Germany to study with the masters. Well, it wasn't just aspiration that got you there, and it wasn't for everybody, especially not for women. Clara should have done it early in her studies, but she had not had the money, and Conrad, her father, could not help her. If you came from a well-off family, and somebody chaperoned you, then a young woman was able to study abroad. Instead, Clara had worked hard to qualify for a stipend to study in New York and later in Boston for a few years. She had had good teachers, but it had been learning the hard way. She had helped Mama and Papa in the Deli, whenever possible to have a little extra money and not to be a burden on her parents. In Boston she had given music lessons to children in one of the private schools. Difficult and financially strained years they had been, but she had succeeded. Clara was proud of what she had achieved.

Staring at the large left-leaning writing on the page, Clara wondered how to respond to Henry's letter. Part of her wanted to accuse him of cruelty towards her sister, but deep in her heart she knew he had suffered, too. He, too, had come to this country with high hopes, and things had started well. But then, all the miscarriages, stillborn children, Baby Lilly surviving only a short time. All the lives not lived, the business threatened, the future uncertain. And yet, did it have to be such a radical step like going back to the village of his youth? Surely there would have been other possibilities. That's what America was all about, opportunity, trying new things, reinventing yourself, even if it was hard. Nobody would have asked what he had done before. But Henry was a proud man, and starting new at the bottom of the ladder after having been his own boss, a business owner, had not appealed to him. That he would deprive Little Henry of his own opportunities, that his son would suffer for his father's decision as well, had never occurred to him. Well, Big Henry always needed to shine. He would be somebody in the old village, claimed that he had returned because he had been homesick, not because of business failure. And he had returned with a modest amount of cash from the sale of his shop and stock of fabrics, tools and machinery, the Singers and the fancy irons. It had bought him more in the old country than it would have in Manhattan.

What Clara really wanted to do, she was convinced at that moment, was to suggest that Big Henry send her nephew back to New York. He could live with her.

Would Henry allow that?

The boy could take classes for young adults in the community center for a while, to make up for what he hadn't learned in that backward village school, and then attend a community college, get the education Elizabeth had wanted for him. Clara could afford it now. Elizabeth had written about Little Henry's rather spontaneous decision to end the apprenticeship with his father. He chose to work in a factory instead of being the object of his father's daily rage. Little Henry didn't want to be another tailor in the family, the fifth generation of Henries to do so, none of them amounting to much of anything with the exception of his father who preserved the aura, over there, of having been the preferred tailor of Manhattan's upper class. But the boy didn't have much of an idea of what he wanted to do instead. Being an unskilled worker surely could not be the solution. It would do for now, Clara thought. At least he would make his own money. The poor little fellow. He was probably feeling quite lost without his mother.

This was all wishful thinking! A single woman with a decent income, yes, but on the road all the time and not really in the position to take care of a boy, almost a young man now whom she hadn't seen for half of his life. And yet . . .

Clara wanted to spin that thought a little longer. *What if?*

She looked around her apartment. She would clear out her study and practice in the bedroom or living room. It was a small room, but he would be comfortable. He probably did not have much, a few clothes, no books, not even a violin. Maybe he had lost his English. It would come back quickly, she was sure of that. She knew enough German though she had not spoken it since her parents died. Most of the time they had talked to her in German, and she and her sister had answered in English. She would be able to communicate with him just fine. Here was the plan. She would write a letter to Little Henry first, suggest the move carefully, feel him out and then wait for his answer before pitching the idea to his father. Her sister would have liked for Little Henry to come back. She would have loved to come back herself, each letter suggested this between the lines, but she didn't have a choice. No choice. Well, Little Henry had a choice, and he had her, his aunt, they would be a family. She hadn't been able to support her sister and her nephew to keep them from following Big Henry, but she could help Little Henry now. The hurdle would be his father's consent. And if he did not give it, Little Henry would have to wait two years until he was 21. Two years. A lot could happen in the meantime. The war would be over, surely. Nobody would care if you were of German descent.

What was she thinking?

Doubts kept creeping into Clara's plans. Maybe the government wouldn't let Little Henry in. But wasn't he still an American citizen? Then they would have to.

Big Henry would never let his son leave. He would have rather broken up his marriage than separate from Little Henry. Was she longing for a son all of a sudden? Did her sister's death make her question her own life choices?

Clara loved her life as a professional musician. Her father had come to this country with a wife and two little daughters, a suitcase each, and a violin, his most precious belonging. His immigration papers, and even the city directory for several years had listed him as "Conrad Schombart, musician." He had exchanged the "K" for a "C" in his first name because people kept misspelling it, but he had not changed the family name of which he had been proud. It sounded a little like "Schubert", the composer he admired. He could never decide if he loved Schubert better than Schumann and named his first-born after Schumann's wife, Clara, an equally, if not more gifted composer and musician than her husband.

Her father had been an old-fashioned man who proclaimed that "a woman can never be better than a man, almost as good, yes, but not better!" And yet, he had allowed Clara to take music lessons, and when she had begged him to let her hold his violin and pluck the strings very carefully, he had allowed it, too. He had wanted to steer her towards the flute because it was considered a feminine instrument, or, better even, the harp, for the same reason. Women looked graceful when playing the harp, like angels, and the rhythmic movements and the positioning highlighted their figures. But Conrad had not been able to afford one. The violin with its curved feminine body resting under a woman's chin, somehow, didn't look right. The violin was supposed to be mastered by a male musician.

Clara had insisted, kept plucking the strings of her father's violin with her little fingers, and broken into tears when he would take it away from her. Conrad, a kind man, wished his girls to be happy, and on her sixth birthday he gave her a violin small enough to hold, and stick it under her little, dimpled chin. You cannot reign in passion, or talent. He had known that only too well. Times were changing, he had been telling himself. Perhaps, Clara would become a music teacher, he had mused, and would work in one

Clara, the aspiring violinist

of the new music schools in which women were trained to teach children how to play an instrument. It was considered part of a good education, even in this country, and it would not scare off any future husbands. It was better than selling bread and cheese in a Deli. Conrad had wanted more for his girls.

Her father had quickly found out that he would not be able to sustain a family on a musician's income. People had hired him for weddings and parties, and the church the family had joined on their block had asked him to play with a group of men and the local *Gesangverein* on Christmas or Easter. What had been a profession in the old country had become a hobby here. Conrad's father had owned a bakery, and he, the second eldest son, had helped out whenever he had needed some extra money, which had been quite often. He had delivered bread and watched his father turn the yellow dough into *Brezel* and *Brötchen*. Being a baker meant getting up in the middle of the night, it was physically exhausting work and the flour you inhaled covered your lungs. Instead of a black lung like the coal miners', bakers had a white lung. Which was worse?

Conrad had not been too keen on that kind of life. Throughout his life, the smell of fresh baked bread had reminded him of his childhood, the smell of home, but also of his father's constant cough. Most importantly, being a baker and getting up at three every morning except on Sundays would not have allowed time for his music. And he had not been able to live without his music, without playing his violin. In need of a steady income, Conrad had gone back to what he knew and opened a small bakery with the little money he had brought from the old country. It had been going so well that he soon had been able to leave the baking to a cousin and open a Delicatessen. *Conrad's Deli* had started small. Yet, since he had been known and respected in the neighborhood not just because of his excellent Pretzels and breads, but also because he played at people's weddings and funerals for free, played everything from folk songs to Schumann and Schubert, it had not taken long for him to build a customer base that helped pay off the loan he had received from an uncle. After a few years he had moved the Deli to a better location and the family to a larger apartment above the new store. Business had been good enough to hire another cousin who freed up a bit of his time so Conrad could still play his music.

Finally, Conrad had had more time to perform in the fancy hotels. He had especially loved playing at the *Dressler*, a luxurious temple with a spacious dining area, potted palm trees and great acoustics. The manager, one of his Deli's customers who loved the English cheddar Conrad had ordered especially for him, had hired him to play during High Tea on Sundays and on special occasions. Conrad would put on his best suit, a starched white collar and his black felt hat and leave the house whistling, looking forward to performing at the *Dressler*. Henrietta, his wife, a smart woman, had let him go without complaining. It would carry Conrad through the week. He would be content. And working side by side in the Deli had given them a lot of time together. Sundays had been special for both of them. Henrietta would often take the girls window shopping at the department stores up in the fashionable part of town or entertain them in the park and buy them sweets from the street vendors. Little treats. And the extra money Conrad had made paid for Clara's music lessons.

Clara placed the letter in front of her on the wooden kitchen table, the same table which her mother, Henrietta, had used to knead the pale dough for the *Maultaschen*. She smoothed the page with both hands. She then picked up her violin, it was like a reflex, and reached for a little basket full of cleaning stuff on the shelf next to the window. She started polishing the blond wood with beeswax and a soft cloth, methodically, lovingly, always along the grain. She missed Conrad and her mother, missed the dinner and music making they had enjoyed together whenever she had returned home from a tour. And now Elizabeth was gone as well. Two sisters, both so different. One determined to become a successful violinist, the other getting married at nineteen, being pregnant for almost a decade, but left with only one surviving child and stuck with a husband who had fallen out of love in the process.

Life's choices, it was all life's choices. Or was it chance? If Elizabeth hadn't met Henry, if her father hadn't been a musician, hadn't brought his violin … Well, this was all futile.

No, Clara did not regret sacrificing a potential husband, nor imaginary children for a career. Was she not living her father's dream of being a professional musician and making a living of it? The places she had been to, the people she had met, the gifted musicians she was playing with, she would not have exchanged that kind of life for anything.

It had been hard, no question, getting to where she was now. Clara remembered the anxiety, but also the excitement of her first years with the New York Ladies' Orchestra, of having been part of the World's Fair in 1893. Musicians, artists, inventors, entrepreneurs all had come to Chicago to present their work at the Columbian Exposition. It was to celebrate the 400th anniversary of Columbus' discovery of the new world, though it took place a year after the actual anniversary because of delays in construction work. And she, Clara, had been part of the World's Fair. Twenty-five years old, it had been her first big concert with the New York Ladies' Orchestra, then as one of several violinists, yet always aspiring to become the first. They had played in the women's pavilion, that prominent white, multi-columned building designed by a female architect to exhibit specifically women's work and creativity. And it did! A library full of books written *by women*, art work, paintings, sculptures made *by women*, and concerts performed and music composed *by women*. It had been a most exciting time. With the invention of electric lights, which beautifully illuminated the fairgrounds, those lights had been switched on by the ladies as well. Clara had devoured all the news about the Fair leading up to the opening, the early plans, the designs. Some journalists had ridiculed the women who had been demanding their own building, and there had been plenty of discussions among women themselves. Should they have their own building, or should women's works be exhibited alongside men's works to show that they were equal in talent and professionalism. But the Lady Managers had insisted on a women's pavilion, and they were proven right.

It had all been there, in full display: Women could be just as creative and successful as men! All they needed was access, the chance to shine, and the Fair provided that. Booked for four weeks that spring, the New York Ladies' Orchestra had played during the opening ceremony, and had two concerts per day, one at mid-day, the other in the late afternoon. Whenever they had not needed to rehearse or perform, Clara had attended lectures or concerts in the women's building. She met other women, artists, community organizers, activists, writers who, like her, had all come to Chicago to meet their "sisters" who were ready for change.

On opening day they waited, in anticipation, for President Cleveland to visit their building. Some of the women had been holding up signs celebrating Queen Isabella, because, without her, Columbus would have never gotten the money nor the ships to go on his famous voyage. But the President never arrived. Instead, he had sent word that he was behind schedule, could not spare the time. It had not exactly been the right message to all the waiting women. They had consoled themselves by saying, "well, the Fair had just started, and there would be another opportunity." They were determined to make the most out of this unique chance to display women's achievements.

Perhaps they had been a bit naïve, Clara thought.

Often strolling along the Midway after the last performance of the day, she had found herself entering a new universe, a cacophony of sound. Street musicians from all parts of the globe had used the World's Fair as a stage. She had wondered how they had been able to travel all the way from South America, Japan or exotic places like Hawaii, home of the Hula, a dance she had not known existed. On the road, they had given concerts, had played on street corners or on boats, sometimes for more than a year. They had slowly made their way to Chicago, always anxious to arrive there on time, meeting other musicians along the way, sometimes teaming up for a spontaneous concert, discovering new tunes and rivalries. How much easier it had been for the members of the New York Ladies' Orchestra who simply had boarded a train and gotten there within twenty-four hours.

The American musicians had caught Clara's interest, especially those hardly seen or heard in the world of white America. While leaving the fairgrounds one evening, she had passed a sideshow, a group of black performers stringing strange notes together, a ragged kind of beat, rhythmic and strangely rousing. She had stopped to listen. This had been a new, a totally new sound, unfamiliar and exciting. The music had made her want to dance, move her feet, swing her upper body, like some of the listeners, but of course she would not, not in public. All she had been able to do was listen, absorb, decipher the strange melodies.

During a break Clara had mustered the courage to approach one of the musicians, a young man who was drying the mouthpiece of his cornet. She had asked him where he was from and what they were playing. Happy that she had shown a genuine interest, he had explained to her the origin of this music, the roots in African folk song, in call-and-response elements sung in the cotton fields and churches. Chicago, he had said, was becoming a center for black musicians, and she should come visit the clubs to meet them. And she had done so, secretly, of course, because even today it wasn't what a young or not-so-young white woman would do, go to all-black clubs often situated in the red-light district where alcohol and sex were being sold. She had asked Johnny, the orchestra's handyman, to come along. Her long black cotton scarf wrapped around her head to hide the face as much as possible and dressed plainly like a working girl who was running an errand, Clara had walked confidently with Johnny towards music town. Standing in front of one of the clubs, their courage had left them, they had not gone inside. But the music had been everywhere, spilled out into the street, filled the night. For a while they had listened to the songs the all-black band had been playing, again that rhythmic, jumping, exciting music she had heard on the Midway. Then they had returned to their dodgy boarding house near Jackson Park, extra careful not to be seen. They would return to music town before their engagement at the Fair ended.

Johnny had to promise Clara to keep their little trips secret, because rules were strict in the New York Ladies' Orchestra: no scandals. Hold up the image of respectability. It was hard enough for female musicians to be taken seriously. A full traveling orchestra had to be extra careful because it was all too easy to make them look like a bunch of cheap women. Clara also had not wanted anybody to think she and Johnny had something going on. Johnny had been as curious about this new music and clearly enjoyed her company, but to her he had been just a young man, a friend, who made life a bit easier for the women on their trips. Over the years, though, whenever Clara visited the city on Lake Michigan, she tried to catch a concert or two in one of the black clubs and to see Scott again, the young cornet player who had introduced her to the music they called Ragtime and who would become one of the great black musicians of his time. This had been a different America, and it still was, with a magical music style born out of Africa, the Caribbean, adapted to the harsh lives of Black America and forever evolving. America, it seemed to Clara, was in the process of becoming itself, not a replica of Europe any more, but a distinct culture. Maybe the next World's Fair, she had wondered back then, would do away with the neo-classical bombast and find its own American style.

Change had been in the air at the Columbian exhibition in Chicago, and yet, the winds had slowed, had not completely died down, but definitely slowed. The fair had closed its doors, the world had abandoned the temporary white city, and two years later the women's building had burnt down with much of the exhibited artwork. The new century had come, its first decade had passed, and the women still organized, still marched, with little progress. It had taken Clara another ten years to become first violinist in the orchestra, still all female. Women composers were the exception and mostly overlooked. The major orchestras did not admit female musicians yet, issued invitations to individual performers occasionally, but this was still very much a man's world.

And yet, if her little sister Elizabeth had only stayed in this big, crazy, always evolving city, things would have turned out to be different for her, Clara thought, looking at the letter in front of her. She could have been one of the artists at the Fair if only she had kept up with her drawing. But it had all been forgotten when she had met Big Henry.

Marriage was meant to provide security, stability, a home. But marriage also meant sex, babies, clearly defined roles. Clara knew a few women who were able to combine both, a career and a family. Educated women who knew how not to have too many babies. Even Clara's life had not been without relationships. She wasn't prudish. But she'd always been careful and discreet about her affairs, and she had definitely put her career first. In Chicago she had learned about birth control in public health lectures in the women's building. It had not all been art and music, but very practical things had been discussed, too. Of course, it had been all under the pretense that the lectures were to prepare young women for a married life, but who was to tell. Clara had even recognized a few girls in the audience from the music clubs she had visited in the red-light part of town who were eager to learn more about how to protect themselves in the job they had been forced into to survive. Somebody had been distributing flyers there, probably the local women's association or the community nurses who were often members. Elizabeth surely would have profited from those lectures. The two sisters had talked about meeting at the Fair. Big Henry, Conrad and Henrietta had planned to come visit as well for a couple days while Clara was playing in Chicago. But, as usual, Henry and her parents had not been able to get away from their shops. And Elizabeth had been unwell because she had been pregnant at the time, again.

Clara's thoughts turned from the past, from things she could not change, to things she could. She thought of her new project, the mixed string quartet, and she thought of Michael. Though still part of the New York Ladies' Orchestra, she had formed a string quartet only a few months ago with Ruth and two men, Michael and Steven, who were excited about playing with such experienced female musicians. Modern men, open-minded, attractive men, too.

Michael's wife had died in childbirth more than two decades ago. She had been too young to have a baby, but they had fallen in love, nothing could have stopped them from getting married. Things had gotten complicated. His story reminded her of Elizabeth who also could not be persuaded to wait, who had known too little, including herself, Clara, all these young women who still knew too little. All she had known was she did not want to be tied down in a relationship. Michael had never remarried, pursued his music career and had been on the road as much as possible during those years. He had kept away from New York and the other life that could have been. He still looked handsome, even though he was in his mid-forties, a few years younger than herself. He understood why she loved the life of a musician. Most of all, he shared her passion for music, for life on the road.

The four of them explored new venues and new music, experimented, discussed things, made plans for small concerts around the country. Maybe they would even make it to Europe, play in Paris, Vienna, Berlin! After all, the great Camilla Urso, whom she had heard play as a child, an inspiration to generations of women musicians, had performed well into her sixties. True, Clara mused, Madame Urso hadn't had the greatest engagements towards the end of her career, playing Vaudeville and being forced to teach to support herself. But times were changing. She was part of a new generation of women musicians. Maud Powell, two years younger than herself, had formed her

Clara, before a concert

own string quartet, and was wildly successful. Of course, Clara admitted to herself, she wasn't quite in the same league. And yet, things were possible now that hadn't been before. It even looked like women would be getting the right to vote in the state of New York this year.

Perhaps if their quartet was successful, she might quit her job with the New York Ladies' Orchestra. It might be time for something new, completely new. In last Sunday's paper she had read about this inventor, Mr. Marconi, whom she had met at one of the city festivals after a concert. He owned a radio factory in upstate New York and was thinking about having regular music programs on the wireless. Maybe he would find the mixed quartet intriguing and their repertoire ranging from folk to classical music and new, distinctly American tunes as well. Well, this was all a bit crazy, but wouldn't it be exciting if her string quartet were to become one of the first to do live broadcasts? They really should decide on a name for it, something catchy, modern, but classy, too. In the article Marconi said the technology was ready, the sound quality improving. Just the thought of sharing your music with the rest of the world was mind-boggling. Elizabeth would have been able to listen to Clara play thousands of miles away. Little Henry still could, if all this worked out and wasn't just another crazy idea in these crazy times. Clara was sure Marconi would remember her. She still had his card.

A chance meeting that might change everything, chance, followed by choice. Clara checked the clock. Almost time to leave for Ruth's place where the quartet would rehearse tonight. They met once a week to play together whenever they were all in town. She loved watching Michael during these rehearsals, loved the passion he showed for new pieces, for trying out different styles. She admired his skills and loved his hands, a musician's hands with long, soft fingers that touched the instrument like a lover. She was careful not to show her feelings because she wasn't sure where this would lead. Her feelings for Michael might lead to a break-up of the quartet or ruin her friendship with Ruth. That would be a high price to pay. She should talk to Ruth, carefully find out how she felt about it and then make a move. Better to be careful.

"What if," she thought again, "I would really live with a man, share his bed officially, travel the world with him, plan a future?" She still had a future, unlike her poor sister. She would visit places, play her music, perform with gifted musicians and friends, maybe conduct an orchestra, cook dumplings and Sauerbraten for her friends.

She would write that letter to Little Henry first thing tomorrow. He had a choice, too, but somebody needed to tell him that. He was almost an adult. He would be on his own soon, but for a little while she could be for him what Elizabeth could not anymore.

Clara folded her brother-in-law's letter neatly into the brown, water-stained envelope. She picked up her violin and gently plucked the strings.

Ruth, Michael and Steven could wait a bit. This moment and song belonged to Conrad, Henrietta and Elizabeth, one of their favorites, a lullaby her father used to play for his two little girls. An old song generations of children knew, here and in the old country, to which Henrietta would sing these timeless lines.

She could hear them.

Der Mond ist aufgegangen …

FIVE
Little Henry II
1967-1968

So this was it, a new life in his seventies, in Omaha, Nebraska. Picture-perfect with his wife, his daughter Toni, her mother-in-law Betty, a dog and two cats. Just without the grandchildren and a son-in-law. Why then wasn't he happy?

He and Katharina were settling in quite well. The house was modern and comfortable, two-stories, the street quiet and lined with trees, about thirty minutes from downtown, by car. They had their own bathroom attached to a large and pleasant bedroom overlooking the fenced-in back yard. Two more people in the house took a bit of getting used to for Betty and Toni, and Katharina and Henry still felt like guests rather than family. But this would change with time. They were developing a daily routine together.

Breakfast was at nine, which Toni set out for them in the kitchen before she left for work. Toast and orange juice, coffee and jam. He only had to put the slices into the toaster so they would be warm, but he just couldn't get them right. They were either popping out pale and barely toasted, or overdone and blackened after he put them back in. A burnt smell would announce his failed experiment to Katharina before she even came downstairs to join him in the kitchen. Surely there was a bakery in town that could produce a good sour dough; after all, quite a number of German immigrants had settled here at the turn of the century.

After breakfast Katharina sorted the dishes into the dishwasher, another new appliance to master, and Henry usually browsed the paper pretending to learn more about his new hometown and refresh his English. He studied the ads, looked at the sports pages, but baseball and football did not quite appeal to him as European soccer did. He also did not understand the rules. His son had been a great goalie in his younger days, and his two grandsons had inherited their father's (not his, he didn't have any!) talent for sports and were great field players. He had often watched their Sunday games when they played the neighboring villages, had sometimes cheered them on, sometimes yelled at them and provided expert commentary together with the rest of the villagers.

Lunch was at one, which Betty, who was a late riser, fixed, something light like a salad, which he hated and called "Hasenfutter" (rabbit food) behind her back, or soup, or a sandwich, which was alright. The midday meal was followed by a nap in one of the big armchairs in the living room. Betty often visited with friends or went shopping, so the house was quiet. In the afternoon, after Toni returned from work, they would all gather in the TV room for their daily dose of television. The routine was as follows: get a cup of instant coffee and a plate of cookies, nestle into your TV chair, prop up your feet and follow the complicated lives of a bunch of rich folks falling in love with the wrong love interest; battling an incurable disease, but saved by a miracle drug; losing or inheriting a fortune and dealing with various complications in their mostly privileged lives. Henry had gotten the hang of it pretty quickly. He pretended he needed a refresher to make up for the decades that he hadn't spoken any English. But fact was, he loved the twisted plots. Katharina sat by, not understanding a word, but content to be with her daughter and allowed to be idle. Toni, happy to have her parents with her, fussed over them and made sure they were comfortable.

So, the typical story of the soap would be something like this: The young, troubled but sensitive doctor meets the beautiful nurse, or patient, or heiress, falls in love, but the situation gets complicated when the young doctor's father, long widowed, pursues the nurse's/ patient's/ heiress' mother who is only in her mid-forties and divorced. The young doctor would have preferred to keep his father out of his own family planning, leave his troubled childhood behind and attach himself to his fiancée's family. But there he was, the patriarch, inserting himself into his son's life once again, the motivation being not so much love for the attractive mother of his soon-to-be daughter in law, but most likely to forge a business alliance, merge financial interests or something like that.

At least in that respect Henry's life had been much simpler. There never had been financial interests to consider. They never had much, not in terms of ambition or money, but they didn't need much of either. Theirs had always been a simple lifestyle. He had had his job in the factory, and in the evenings they had been doing some extra work at home assembling parts of electrical fuses for his factory to pay for Toni's secretary school. They had owned the old farmhouse, which had always needed some repair, but there had been no money for that. It had not really bothered them. At least not until Willi, their son, had gotten married and his wife begun to change everything around them, had Willi install a bathroom, linoleum floors and built-in cupboards in the big kitchen that used to be Heinrich's tailor shop.

And, yet, his own story wasn't that far off from a soap opera plot, Henry mused. He couldn't quite concentrate on the slowly developing story today. The question kept nagging him: Why wasn't he happy?

Here he was trying to turn the clock back. It had been one of the great regrets of his life not to have returned to America when he was young. He saw it as a missed opportunity. Regret – maybe it was too strong a word. That feeling he had stored away deep inside was like a family heirloom, or a faded photograph you find quite unexpectedly while looking for your spare glasses in the back of a drawer or on a crowded shelf. You pick it up, smooth it a bit, not so much as to straighten it out, but to stop the time, to linger and ponder what once was. Before you get too melancholic and unwrap not just the memory of a moment, but possibly the heartache of a life, you put it back and pretend to forget about it.

For a strange moment, Henry felt like the ten-year-old again, his brain opening one of the long-sealed drawers and conjuring up that longing for what once had been, the "good" part of his childhood in another country, this country. After a while, the home he had been forced to leave had felt like another world, a distant memory of a time when his mother and father had gotten along, and grandparents and aunt doted on him, of family gatherings and walks in the park.

Henry gave himself credit. He had made a real effort to fit into his new life in his father's hometown, a small village in Germany. He was liked by most, even today, had made friends, found his place in the community because his father's side of the family had lived there forever. But then his mother had died unexpectedly leaving that huge gap, a hole in his heart which he thought could never heal. Out of his loneliness came the need to reclaim the happier years, and he had thought about reconnecting with her part of the family in America. With his grandparents dead, there had still been Aunt Clara who had been in touch with his mother regularly. After her death, Clara had written to him directly, still calling him Little Henry, had asked how he was and if he missed her. She had even suggested that he come back and live with her.

Her kindness had confused him even more. Where did he belong? It was this question he had banned from his mind long ago that now haunted him again. He could have decided it back then, about five decades ago. He had tried, even taken the first steps by going to the post office in his village, getting the address of the U.S. Consulate in Frankfurt, requesting the paperwork and applying for a passport, an American passport. With the forms all filled out and his father's signature forged, because Henry was still under age, he had taken the train to Frankfurt, where he had never been before, for an interview with the Consular officer. The officer had been friendly, but a bit suspicious. Where was his father, he had asked, or his mother? Henry had produced a few tears, which had not really been hard, and had told him that since his mother's death his father had been ill. The officer had signed the provisional passport, after all, the boy had been born in the U.S., stamped it and then explained that he would have to return to America to reclaim his citizenship within a year. For that he would need his father's permission. At least this was how Henry, who had been a bit nervous and therefore had not caught all of it, had remembered the procedure. In 1918, the Great War had been coming to an end, travel had not been possible yet. So he had waited while the precious document had kept him from getting drafted for the final months of the war. He was an American citizen.

Decisions. He had tried to avoid making decisions all his life. He had ended the apprenticeship with his father when his mother had still been alive, but he had felt at the time that his father had been relieved he had done so. He would have been a lousy tailor. But when he finally had mustered the courage to make another big decision, he had let the opportunity to leave slip away. He had never responded to Aunt Clara's letters, so she had not known that he had been contemplating a return. But how would he have told Heinrich that he was going to leave him and the village to go back to Manhattan, let alone get his permission? After a while Clara's letters had stopped, and Henry, in his passivity, had accepted this as a sign.

Maybe he was being too hard on himself, Henry thought while readjusting the pillow behind his back. He recalled one of his grandmother's pieces of wisdom: "If one door closes, another opens." He had never been the one to open doors for himself, but when he saw an opportunity, he had managed to walk through. Things had often happened in spite of his inaction. He had always been a bit of a drifter, but a clever one, and through a bit of scheming in the background, by weaving a net of stories here and there, he had influenced some decisions others had made along the way. Occasionally, good things had happened even without any scheming. He had fallen in love, just like in a cheesy soap opera.

Katharina, the black-haired little woman with the cute slightly upturned nose, which made her look impish, and Henry, the Ami, had met at a dance in the village hall. The war had been fought mainly outside of German borders.

In spite of the rationings and the ragged young men coming back from the battlefields and prison camps in France and elsewhere, shell-shocked and branded for life, village life had somehow preserved some normalcy. Boys had still met girls and vice versa, some of them had managed to fall in love, maybe because they really fell for the girl, or because the girl's father owned a winery. Some girls had gotten pregnant and then married. Katharina, half-orphaned like himself and living with her mother, had known she wanted to be with Henry pretty quickly. After the dance they had met again at the wine festival in Rauenthal, and then the carnival in Eltville. She had liked his softness, his need for her. She had seen the hurt in his bright blue eyes. They had dated for a few months, met regularly in the little square in the middle of the village where the young had been hanging out on Sunday after church under the watchful eyes of the elders who often put a pillow in their window frame to rest their arms on comfortably for their weekly entertainment.

Sometimes Henry and Katharina had gone for walks in the vineyards, which had been a bit more complicated because of her mother's warnings that the neighbors might gossip. On one of those lovely walks to their favorite spot up on the hill on the outskirts of the forest from where they could see all the way to the big city's cathedral spires beyond the river on a clear day, Henry had talked about leaving for America. He had described his Manhattan, the vendors, the Italian and Jewish neighborhoods, the big park and department stores, the harbor full of ships spewing out newcomers and taking on cargo to be shipped all across the world. He had pulled out an envelope and a pencil stub and drew his old street, the house where he used to live, his grandparents' Deli. It all had felt so real at that moment. Surely Aunt Clara would welcome Katharina, would help them get started. He would be turning twenty-one next summer and did not need his father's permission any more.

But the moment had passed. Katharina, a simple, but practical girl, had listened sympathetically, but she could not picture herself leaving her mother. Henry had known what it meant to leave loved ones behind. So he had decided to drop the topic for the moment, had folded the envelope neatly into a small square and stuffed it into his coat pocket. Maybe his aunt would not want him to bring a wife anyway. Holding Katharina's small, rough hand, he had felt a warmth in his heart and belly that he had not felt in a long time. So he had done what he usually did: postpone the decision. And after a few years with two children born four years apart, he had pushed his memories into his mind's deepest drawer and closed it. A family of four would have been quite a surprise for Aunt Clara, more than she would have bargained for. From then on Henry never talked about his mother, his early childhood in Manhattan and the relatives he had left behind.

Henry watched Toni who had changed into her comfy, but stylish pants and soft sweater, while still wearing her office make-up and jewelry. Nibbling on her cookies and analyzing the enfolding story of the handsome widower charming his son's mother-in-law, she looked up and said: "Can you believe it? I'm losing track who's dating whom. Wasn't she still seeing her ex-husband?"

Henry loved his daughter more than anybody in the world, maybe because they had spent so much time apart. She had left for America at the age of twenty, and he had encouraged her to leave. She never saw him for what he was, but only for what he was to her. In her eyes, he could do no wrong. In his eyes, she stayed forever young and beautiful. She was the one who had moved to his old home country, who had claimed the citizenship he had given up and who had turned into this elegant American woman successful in her job and much liked by her circle of friends. In an accident she had lost a husband before they could have children, but she and Betty had helped each other through the grief. She had built a life for herself, and now she even had her parents live with them. To Toni, this completed her family. To Henry, it somehow did not feel right. That feeling would pass, surely. They had only arrived a couple months ago. What had he expected?

"Go figure," Henry said to Toni, trying out expressions he had not heard or used in a lifetime while thinking that life wrote the strangest stories. Only die-hard soap opera fans would believe *his* story. Big Henry had messed with his life just like the patriarch with the young doctor's.

When the weather had gotten colder and meeting outside in the vineyards or the small marketplace was not exactly a pleasure anymore, Henry had told his father, Heinrich, that he and Katharina were planning to get engaged before Christmas and married the following summer. Katharina had nudged him gently to make a decision as she had wanted things to feel and be settled.

She never had any doubts, even to this day, never questioned how life had turned out for her, just accepted it, Henry thought. She had accepted him the way he was. She trusted him, except with money. She had always carried her purse in the pocket of her apron, like a kangaroo, keeping his weekly wages safely secured. She knew him too well and his love for cigars and cognac. She would not even leave the purse unprotected when she had to use the outhouse. He chuckled when he recalled her screaming "Henriiii" at the top of her voice when her precious purse had slid out of the apron, which she flipped over when settling on the seat. It went right down the toilet. Literally down the drain it had gone, in slow motion disappearing into the open sewer behind the outhouse, staying on the surface and then going under. What to do?

Henry bravely had pulled on his rubber boots, taken the pitchfork and waded into the smelly basin. He always found the purse, never yelled at his wife, just kept muttering "nah, nah, nah," and "eijajei …" Katharina had waited close by, yet at a safe distance with a handkerchief in front of her nose and mouth. She waited impatiently for him to crawl out of the sewer and rinse off the leather purse. She would immediately snatch the purse from him, rinse the coins and carefully wash the paper bills herself in soapy water to then string the bills on the clothesline to dry while keeping a watchful eye on them. The final act had been to iron the bills to make them look like new. Katharina loved ironing money and always did when she gave the grandchildren a ten-Mark bill for their birthdays. The bills then felt so new and crisp.

Heinrich had had no objections to having a woman in the house again. The household clearly needed one. Little Henry could have done worse, Heinrich had thought, especially after he had met Rosa, Katharina's mother. Heinrich had not liked life as a widower. So he had made his wishes clear. He would give his consent to the engagement under one condition: that Katharina's widowed mother would marry him. Henry would not only have a new wife and mother-in-law, but a stepsister and a stepmother at the same time. Rosa had agreed, because Heinrich could still turn on the charm, had a business, a house and provided some security. She, too, could have done worse.

Everything had been settled by Christmas followed by a modest double wedding in the summer of Little Henry's twenty-first birthday. Heinrich had commanded the stage when it should have been the young couple's big day, but Henry had been used to that. Heinrich had seemed happy for the first time in years, and that had been enough for his son. It had taken the pressure off of him and allowed him to make a bold move. The young couple, husband and wife as well as stepbrother and stepsister, had decided not to move in with their father, stepfather and father-in-law; mother, mother-in-law and stepmother. They had found a little apartment in the village next to Henry's factory and enjoyed just being together. Those had been happy times for the young couple, and even for Heinrich and his new wife Rosa. But they were not to last.

The whole village had gossiped about Rosa's pregnancy, pregnant even before the daughter! In her forties! And people had felt justified in their judgement that sex was for the young. The "old", especially the women, they believed, should refrain from sex. In truth, they had been envious of Rosa because their own marriages had long cooled. As if having been punished for her frivolity, the poor woman had died in childbirth barely a year after the wedding. Heinrich had been devastated. This great loss had reminded him of his first marriage with Elizabeth and all the children they had lost, except Little Henry. Fate had provided a cruel twist to the familiar story, though: this time the child had survived, a little boy, but not the mother.

For Heinrich this had been final proof that life had punished him, yet, he didn't really know for what. He started to be completely withdrawn. From that moment on he had lived in his workshop and spent time in the pub down the street. He had had no interest in family or friends any longer; and he had pushed the young couple to take care of the infant. While Henry, as usual, had not been keen on making such a life changing decision on raising his own stepbrother, Katharina had held her ground and resisted. She could not forgive the child the loss of her beloved mother. They had, however, made one concession: a move back into the farmhouse, a decision that Henry would regret many times in the years to come. The baby had been given to Rosa's brother, Katharina's childless uncle, in the village up the hill. A substantial amount of money had sweetened the deal, and that was that. The poor kid, not wanted by his father nor stepbrother, would die at eighteen in the early days of World War II, the war his stepbrother Henry did not have to fight because he still insisted on being an American.

Henry's eyes wandered across the room. He just could not concentrate on the television program today. He looked out the large front window. Omaha. It was certainly not New York. No life in the streets, no vendors, no heavy traffic, just the milkman, the postman and the kid throwing the daily newspaper from his bike onto the porch. A Midwestern city you could only navigate with a car, but he did not drive. He was too old to ride a bike now, and nobody did anyway, nor did people go for a walk. Some streets did not even have sidewalks. The choices were limited: you either visited somebody, or people would come to your house. There needed to be a purpose in heading out to do anything: shopping, visiting, maybe walking the dog—one of his chores that forced him to leave the house before breakfast. Toni would take out the "beast" for a second walk after dinner.

Toni's and Betty's friends were pleasant people, but they made Henry feel uncomfortable. They felt no connection to each other; there was nothing to talk about, no shared history. They asked politely how he liked Omaha, if he missed his German relatives and the old home, and veered off quickly when he started talking about his grandchildren; how old they were, that the boys were good at soccer and the girls liked their own rooms in their new house at the southern end of the village. Henry was proud of his son Willi, though he had never told him. Willi had built that house by himself after work, stone by stone, for three years including weekends in a neighborhood where new plots had been auctioned off by the village for which vineyards and strawberry fields had been cleared. But Henry also felt a little envious and some resentment, as if the old house had not been good enough for the family. Though they all would continue to live in the same village just fifteen minutes apart, on foot, he still had felt abandoned. He had conveniently forgotten that he only would have had to sign the house over to his son so Willi could apply for special family loans for the modernization. But he hadn't done so because Henry never trusted anybody, and Katharina, as usual, had agreed. So they would stay behind in the old house. That was when he had started to plant an idea into Toni's head: to bring him and Katharina to America.

He had done it subtly. Toni, over the years, had often suggested they live with her, but given up on the idea eventually. In his weekly letters to Toni, Henry had described the prospect of staying in that old house by themselves without his son's family: he would have to do all the chores, could not expect Katharina to do a whole lot because of her diabetes, which, eventually, would only worsen. It was alright, he had written, because Willi and his wife would still come by and help with the shopping. But they couldn't count on them being around all the time. What if they both got worse, who would look after them? He then would write about more cheerful things, give Toni the village gossip, and, at the end of each letter, he stressed that she should not worry too much about them. He and Katharina would manage …

It had taken about six months to guide Toni towards making their move a reality. She had arranged for all the paperwork and, together with her brother, found a buyer for the old house. It had sold at a fraction of the price they had hoped for. Toni had divided up the money with one third going to Henry and Katharina, another to cover the expenses for the move, and one third to her older brother Willi, who could use the money for the new house. Toni had flown in, put some of the furniture in storage and sorted out a household of fifty years. Most of it had to go, and there had been nothing of value, really. The red velvet two-seater from the living room and two large pictures that had been hanging over her parents' bed for as long as she could remember, would be part of her brother's move to the new house in a couple months. Had they not been brought over from Manhattan by her grandmother? She could not recall talking much about her with her father. It would have been ironic to bring them back to America, but Toni had never been sentimental. It had been enough for her to know that they would not end up on the trash heap.

"I'm going out for a smoke," Henry told the women gathered around the TV, pulled on his slippers and straightened his suspenders. Toni hated it when he smoked in the house, though he sometimes did in his bathroom with the window open. But she made sure he had a supply of his stubby cigars. Out on the deck in the back yard, Henry bit off the end and spit it into an ashtray on the cast iron garden table. He just couldn't get used to using the cigar cutter Toni had given him. He lit a match, slightly roasted the end of the cigar until it glowed and slowly puffed to keep it going. His medicine was running out, which worried him. Not the one for high blood pressure, for which he could get a prescription from the local pharmacy, but his feel-good-drops, as he called them. The old family doctor at home had first prescribed them after a bike accident in which Henry had hurt his back. The pain had been intense, and he had needed a strong pain killer. Henry liked the feeling of those pain killers, the slight numbness and comfort he had experienced. In order to keep the prescription coming, he had told the doctor that his pain was not going away. After a while his body had needed those drops, he became addicted and to avoid any issues, the doctor had kept quietly prescribing them. Here in Omaha, Henry had no idea how to get them and did not want to admit to Toni how dependent he was on them.

Henry kept a correspondence going with the family who had bought the farmhouse. Much had changed. Henry learned that the courtyard where his grandchildren used to play, had been partly closed off and turned into the carpenter's shop. The place was being renovated some, but his old apartment over the entrance was still vacant and nothing had been done to it yet. Henry liked the carpenter's wife, Susanna, and her two young, raucous boys. He kept sending them and his grandchildren postcards of cowboys and Indians, though there were none around in Omaha, at least not that he knew. He had never seen any. The only remnants of the past were in the name Omaha.

The men's choir had come on the evening before their departure and sung the familiar songs as a farewell. "Muss I denn zum Städtele hinaus …" Though he had never cared for that song, even when Elvis had recorded it as a tribute to his time in Germany as a G.I., Henry had gotten misty-eyed. He had been a choir member since his sixteenth birthday, loved the old folk songs and the male company, the gossiping after rehearsal and a glass of wine or two down at Else's place. His grandchildren had not really grasped yet that their grandparents were to leave for good. Willi had been happy for them, but parting had not been as easy as they both had anticipated. They had never talked much, watched soccer together or some other T.V. program, but he was a good boy, quiet and dependable, though he had inherited his grandfather's love for drink. Neighbors had sent them off with best wishes. Henry, the Ami, was going home. No turning back. So he had done it, he had returned to the home country, though so many years later than planned. Well, not exactly home, not to New York, Manhattan, but at least to America. Omaha.

He should write to Susanna. What if they couldn't find renters for his old apartment? She clearly needed the money. Hadn't Katharina mentioned just the other day that she had always expected to be buried in the village graveyard overlooking the valley? That she would have to look at an American graveyard in Toni's neighborhood now, so she could imagine where they would take her. That it would probably be alright as well because everything seemed well kept, though a bit foreign, and Toni would visit her grave. He might have mentioned it to Toni, assuring her that her mother would be fine, that, maybe, she felt a bit homesick, but he sure did not … That, maybe, she missed the grandchildren, but wouldn't want to tell Toni. No, he, Henry, was fine, he liked living with Toni and Betty. Well, he did sometimes wonder if it had been the right decision for Katharina. No, Toni shouldn't worry too much. Katharina would adjust. Weaving another net of stories …

A year later Katharina and Henry moved back, quietly, into their old apartment. The men's choir did not serenade them upon arrival, and the village folks simply said: "Ei, seid Ihr wieder da? (So, you're back)" and went their ways. As if that interlude had not taken place.

Susanna liked the old people, took a good portion of Henry's pension and a refund from the purchase of the house so they would not have to pay rent. She cooked and cleaned for them. And when Katharina died a few years later, Henry still had Susanna. She made sure he felt at home, took his medicine including the "feel-good-drops". Henry felt content, at least most of the time and especially enjoyed when Susanna flirted with him. She knew how to make him laugh.

* * * * *

1981

Sitting in his wheelchair on the front porch, Henry enjoyed the afternoon sun. Susanna and her family were on vacation, so he was staying with Willi and his daughter-in-law for a few weeks. It was OK, but Henry disliked feeling like a guest although they did do everything to make him feel welcome. His youngest granddaughter was expected back from a year abroad at a Florida college. She had visited with Toni who, in the meantime, had left Omaha to start a new life in a new home in the Ozarks. It seemed to run in the family, the attraction to America.

Henry picked up a large red checkered kitchen towel he had come to use instead of a hanky and wiped his eyes. A hanky got wet too quickly, and his eyes kept watering. Old age, he thought, what's good about getting that old? He was almost twice the age of his mother when she died, the woman who had never felt at home in this village nor in this country. Where did he belong? He had moved back to the village for Katharina's sake, hadn't he? Toni had finally understood that. And she had made that decision for him to bring them back, hadn't she? She still had Betty and now a second husband, the guy he never really liked. Nobody was good enough for Toni. She probably had a new dog by now and, as always, a couple cats. She wasn't alone.

Decisions. He had never been good at them. But it had all worked out alright, hadn't it? He could not wait to get back to his own apartment, his own routine with Susanna without the daily showers and shaves his son helped him with, which was fine with him. Though he did not own the place anymore, it was in the old farmhouse where Henry felt close to Katharina and his mother, though she had not been happy there. His thoughts turned to the past. What else was there? Certainly no future. That belonged to the young. Henry unfolded the kitchen towel and wiped his eyes. It was getting wet.

SIX
The Bay Window
2012

Did you know that hummingbirds are killers? No, not the ones visiting my bird feeder every day. When they drink from that sweet red liquid, they beat their delicate wings like tiny helicopters. They are probably domesticated, like my cats, who still have claws and sharp teeth but do not fight over food. They know I will feed them, more than is even good for them.

They are curious creatures, these hummingbirds, in more ways than one. When I strain my ears, I can hear the sound their little feathery wings are making. A faint buzz. They hover over the feeder, insert their long slender beak into the feeding tube, stay very steady, better than any helicopter pilot possibly could. I swear they sometimes pause and look back to check out the person behind the windowpane. I wonder what they see. Holding up my binoculars as an extension of my eyes, I probably look like an alien. But isn't that what I am to them anyway, a creature so different from them, wingless, white haired, old, mostly stationary, sitting in this big old leather chair, feet propped up? What we share is that I'm just as curious about them as they seem to be about me. But they can simply take off, find another source of sugar, maybe bright green, on a neighbor's porch, another land of plenty for them. No loyalties here.

It's the truly wild ones somewhere in South America that fight over food, or potential mates. Then their beak turns into a deadly weapon tearing into the tiny breast of another brightly colored hummingbird. I read about it in one of my bird books that I keep stacked next to me, on the little round coffee table. And did you know they have forked tongues? Just like snakes. They don't suck the liquid through their beak, no, they curl their forked tongue against the inside of their beak, trap that sweet, tempting source of energy, the fuel they need to beat their gossamer wings. *Gossamer wings*, wasn't there a song? Something about a trip to the moon?

How can such beautiful birds be so ferocious? Survival. That's what it's all about. Passing on the stronger genes. As delicate as these tiny creatures appear, they are tough little fighters, survivalists. When food is scarce, you know, they can slow down their heart rate and metabolism, conserve energy, almost reach a state like hibernation, a deep, deep sleep. Amazing, isn't it? If only humans could do that when they go hungry. This way we could probably live forever.

Why am I telling you all this when you aren't even here? I guess, that's what old people do, watch birds and talk to themselves. Or chat with people who are not around. Even occasionally with the dead. No, it's not all I do, and I haven't lost my mind, yet. I read a lot, mostly romance. And I listen to books on tape when my eyes get tired. It's just not as easy to skip the slippery parts of the stories because you don't see them coming, can't glance at the next paragraph and turn that page quickly to continue reading a few paragraphs down. I wasn't always that prudish, you know. And maybe that's not really what it is. Reading about intimacy, sex really, brings back memories I'd rather not have.

It's really none of your business, you know, so don't ask me about them.

I know you liked the view from my big bay window when you visited. You were a college student the first time you came, a lovesick one. You went to the mailbox by the road every morning to check if that boy you knew from your history class had written. You were hoping to meet him before going home because there had been the potential for romance. But it had been the end of the term. He was to go on a study abroad trip to England, and you were to travel towards the west coast and then visit us before returning to Germany. He never wrote.

And then, several years later, you came with your boyfriend who dropped you off on the way to visit his folks in Kansas and returned a week later. Ted didn't think he was the right one for you, but he wouldn't say anything because he liked you. I know yours was a bright young man, a graduate student, just like you. He was good-looking, too, tall, blond, a swimmer's chest, though he could have dressed a little better. I've always liked well-dressed men. But your young man was very casual, his Birkenstocks looked like a dog had been chewing on them, his khaki-colored shorts were faded and his T-Shirt ripped under the armpit. He had stuffed his extra clothes and toothbrush in a brown paper bag. As if he was trying to make absolutely sure that the only relatives you had in this part of the world wouldn't take him for your future husband. I saw your face when he got out of the car. You were happy he came, but you saw what I saw, a young man not ready to commit, desperately trying *not* to impress. I should have talked to you about the sleeping arrangements then. I'm sorry I didn't. We knew the two of you were moving in together after the summer, but Ted wasn't comfortable about both of you sleeping in the guest room downstairs. I shouldn't have left it to you to bring up the subject. It surely didn't help how Ted felt about your young man.

I saw how the boys at the check-out in the supermarket looked at you while stuffing groceries into brown paper bags, the same bags your boyfriend used as an overnighter. Young men used to look at me like that when I was your age. And I liked it. Your young man, he didn't look at you like that. He should have, because you were beautiful, smart, lovely. Just as I was back when I first met these cool, carefree American soldiers who finally, finally had ended this dreadful war. If only I could have gone into hibernation, or the hummingbirds' deep sleep during these grey years that had left us hungry and worried, worried about my brother, your father. Willi had been drafted right out of school. The difference between you and me was that I knew that I was beautiful, the boys didn't need to tell me. You didn't in spite of all your education. I should have told you. But I never learned to be a woman's woman, or a mother. For a long time I only knew how to be the competitor.

You know, Table Rock Lake reminds me so much of the Rhine valley, though it's actually much more spectacular and rugged here. It's why I fell in love with the spot when Ted and I were looking for a site to build a house together. The area used to be much more isolated when we first moved in, but in a good way. You couldn't see the neighbors from up here. There were only a few houses hidden among the trees. It felt like we were in the middle of a forest sloping down to the lake, that beautiful, dark blue lake. The raccoons are still coming up to the house at dusk. I watch them from the kitchen window, love it when they busily wash their little hands in the well, you just need to make sure they don't get into the trash, and there is also a fox family that strolls by in the mornings. No, I don't feed them. They are wild animals after all, and I like them wild. I was quite wild myself, fiercely independent, you know. I always knew what I wanted.

Back then my hair was dark, almost black. It has turned thin and white, but you can't tell because I hide it under this magnificent silver-haired wig, real hair, mind you, that Joanie, my hairdresser back in town, had made for me. It's piled up high, 60s style, just like Audrey Hepburn would do her hair, though hers was her own, deep black and carefully designed around her beautiful face. I always wanted to look like her, even followed her various haircuts, long, piled up, loose around the shoulders, and real short. She was like a graceful doe. I never take my wig off in company. I still have my pride. But these days company is the cleaning woman and the nurse checking in to see if I have a sufficient supply of my medication and haven't fallen off the porch.

Sundays are special, though, when Nancy stops by after she's walked the dogs on the way down to her house. I always keep a bottle of bubbly in the fridge, and I ration the pralines you send me for Christmas, the ones filled with liqueur which you can't buy here. I keep them in the freezer and take them out, two for Nancy, two for me, every Sunday. Chocolate filled with alcohol somehow doesn't go together in this country. What if your kids decide to go through that special candy box? You could probably be accused of harming your child and go to jail for it. Funny, when I grew up in that wine region of yours, they let us taste the new wine, not yet all fermented but sweet and with an earthy taste. Everybody laughed when this made us run to the outhouse in the courtyard. Nancy and I always have a great time and love the special treats we share, just like teenagers. Sundays are good.

Toni, looking pretty in an army jacket

I've always been petite, and back when I was your age or a bit younger, I was really thin with dark black hair reaching down to my shoulders. I used to curl it with paper strips cut from the newspaper, twist the strands of hair around them and tie the ends of the paper strip together. I'd moisten the curls just a tiny bit with a dish cloth, not too much so the paper strips wouldn't get soggy, and then have them dry overnight. It made nice curls and was less damaging to the hair than a curling iron, but it took all night to look good for the next day. I just loved those electric curlers Betty gave me when I got here. You put them in for twenty minutes and you were ready to go out.

I was quite bright and a quick learner, definitely eager to get out of that village where everybody knew each other and nobody forgot anything. Life didn't offer a lot of prospects for a young woman there in the late forties. But I was no *Sister Carrie*, you know that girl from the novel. I read that book years ago. She leaves her small town to find work in the city. I always found her quite naïve. She doesn't find work, has no skills or education to speak of, maybe she gives up too easily, I don't know, but she ends up with several men, one after the other. I forgot most of the plot, but what really stuck with me is the image at the end of the novel: Carrie in a rocking chair, alone in an apartment paid for by one of her lovers, thinking about how she got there, rocking back and forth, in constant motion, yet going nowhere.

No, it's not how I feel about my life. My parents, poor as they were, granted me a better start than Carrie ever had, an education even better than my brother's who was the smartest kid in school. Papa felt Willi was strong enough to work in the factory. But of me, little Antonia, they had to take care and so they sent me to trade school. I've always made my own money, you know. Make sure you always do as well. Don't become dependent on anybody. It wasn't a great job I had after I left school. I had to do the required social year first, everybody had to, but I worked for our village teacher, helped him with school stuff. Others were not so lucky. Your mother was sent to a farm in the east, Czechoslovakia, I believe, and had to work really hard. They treated the kids like slaves. But Papa found a way to keep me at home. Then I did my apprenticeship as an office clerk in the big winery where they made all that champagne, maybe that's why I like my bubbly so much. When production was cut, I was sent to work in the electric supply factory where Papa worked. We were essential for the war effort, or whatever they called it, but at least we got paid – if ever so little. The girls in production got laid off after the war ended and the men came back to reclaim their positions. I was kept on because I knew how to type and do shorthand. What boring work I was doing then, and yet, I was luckier than others. Riding my bike to work along the country road, I dreamed of flying away, getting out of that stuffy village, moving to a city with theaters and clubs, shops, different people, different men.

You would have liked Bobby. And, yes, before you ask, fact is, I wouldn't be here if it hadn't been for Bobby. In my memory he is forever young. His smile, his unruly hair, the cigarette hanging from his lips, to me he looked like a movie star. He wasn't as tall as my brother, but I only reached up to his shoulders, his broad shoulders. I loved it when he held me …

He came with the American troops to the region, ending years of war that had drained the village of our young men, but luckily, left it mainly untouched. Most of the bombs had been dropped across the river. I remember the sky turning red. What attracted me to Bobby was that he was wild. They say he was the black sheep of his family, a fairly wealthy family in the Midwest. I didn't know this when I first met him, but I guessed that he came from a good home when he showed me photographs of his mother. She was wearing pearls, real pearls, not fake things like mine from the black market. His mother was holding a cocktail glass. And then the photos of his house! A large, modern farm, which was set back from a street lined with tall trees. I fell in love not just with Bobby, but with that photograph of his home, that street, the white fence, that open landscape right on the outskirts of Omaha.

Bobby was so different from the young men I had gone to school with. They now returned, one by one, from the war looking gaunt and grey, older than their actual age. What had they done? What had they seen? Many didn't return at all. Like Peter, the policeman's son, the biggest Nazi in the village. He had forced his only son, Peter, to join the SS, a sweet kid really who used to play the accordion at the village Weinfest. He talked about studying music and playing in an orchestra. He was the first boy I ever kissed, back behind the stage. It was a sloppy wet kind of kiss, neither of us knew how to do it properly, but it was sweet. Maybe it was for the better he didn't come back.

Well, it was easier not to talk, to pretend these grey looking fellows who either just sat there staring holes into the air or couldn't sit still, always moving about, not talking, none of them talking, were still the same carefree schoolboys. Nobody was overweight. Few had jobs. Yet, by and large, the American troops treated them well, even gave them the odd job here and there. In fact, once they discovered that Papa spoke English, they recruited him as an interpreter. They would hang out in our kitchen as they came through—to see him, and me, the *Fräulein*. There was no shortage of young Americans in my home. That's when the other girls kept showing up, some of them friends from school or work. They would pretend they were visiting me, but I knew that they just wanted to have a look at these American boys, perhaps get a cigarette, maybe some nylon stockings, a date. I made sure they didn't interfere with my young man.

Why is all this coming back to me today, and why am I telling you about these long-gone days? Memory is a tricky thing. We re-shape it every time we remember. What is real? What do we want to believe? Was I just like those hummingbirds going for the sweet nectar, beautiful and mesmerizing, yet ready to take on whatever was in my way?

Papa was surprised that he could understand these American soldiers. He had forgotten the language of his childhood. With his mother dead there simply was no connection to his past. It had not mattered anymore. But finally it did again, and he felt important, had skills nobody else had in this cow town. He was not just an untrained factory worker any more. Papa was much smarter than most people suspected. He was sly, had avoided being drafted in either one of the big wars, claiming he was an American citizen although he had given up his passport long ago. He had gotten away with it. Listening to these young Americans, Papa's memories, long stored away, pushed to the forefront. He mentioned his birthplace, a busy city with buildings touching the sky, where life had somehow been larger and Sunday trips to the park with his parents part of the weekend ritual, but he didn't tell me much. His English was coming back quickly, and I picked it up from him. I've always had a talent for languages, and it helped me when I started working for that German language newspaper in Omaha, where both languages were useful. The GIs liked my funny-looking, little, middle-aged Papa with the round glasses and the Hitler moustache. He shaved it off quickly when the Americans came. He didn't need to pretend that he was sort of a supporter anymore, though foreign born.

There had been others before Bobby, but nothing serious, really. Just play. The villagers must have talked about me, just as they talked about other girls who were going out with GIs. But you know what, I didn't care. I had survived the war, and I knew what I wanted. I had my revenge when I went back to visit Mama and Papa, Willi and you all. I made sure to look the part of the elegant woman from America who, obviously, had made it.

Bobby was as daring and reckless as I was. We were so young! And we wanted so desperately to move on. Back then, in the old country, Bobby took me to clubs in Wiesbaden where live bands played Jazz and Swing, those hot rhythms went right through my body, touching me, where nobody else had touched me until I met him. Such music had been forbidden during all those dark years. All this carefree dancing, drinking, yes, smoking, loving, it all promised an easy life and helped forget the past. Bobby was an excellent dancer. Wearing dark Marlon Brando sunglasses and sometimes dressed in a black leather jacket, keeping that army cap slightly tilted or wearing his uniform jacket unbuttoned when his superiors weren't around, he looked the part of the romantic, yet tough, suitor. And he made me feel beautiful, attractive, seductive even. I knew how to keep him interested. I watched the girls, the ones who were most liked, who somehow seemed special, a bit aloof, and the others who flirted as well, and eventually "made the rounds". I made sure not to become one of them.

And all the trips we took in that battered army jeep. I would call in sick, or bribe my boss with cigarettes and just take off with Bobby. There seemed to be no rules, no boundaries. We drove up the Rhine valley,

Arriving from America, visiting "home": Toni, nieces, Katharina and Henry

and then on to Garmisch, I had never seen such high mountains, just the two of us, crossing a country full of scars left by a horrible war whose memory would stay on the minds of the people forever. Bobby didn't care about non-fraternization laws and raised eyebrows. He wanted to impress me, the dark-haired smiling girl from the village, and my parents didn't object. They never denied me any pleasures, especially those that didn't cost them anything and brought them extra rations of coffee and chocolate.

Finally, life was exciting. This is what being young, carefree, means, isn't it? Have you ever felt this kind of exhilaration? Probably not, because you never experienced what we went through. All of a sudden everything seemed possible. Not worrying about where to get groceries for your next meal, who is talking about you behind your back, and if your brother is ever coming home. I remember posing for snapshots in the grass or by the car on a country lane with beautiful scenery in the back to make sure Bobby wouldn't forget me when he left Germany. He spoiled me with presents none of the villagers could afford and with his quick laugh, good looks and American coolness, he seemed to offer everything I was looking for in a man. I really loved him with a deep

Smashing Bobby

passion, a feeling I never had again after his death, not with the guys I dated occasionally, and not with Ted. Ted was a different kind of love. But at least I had experienced it: Passion.

That's why I skip the love scenes in the novels I read, because they remind me of what I once had, what I lost. Don't ask any questions. I told you it's really none of your business. But, yes, you are right, I know what you are thinking: Bobby was also my way out.

I wasn't worried too much when he shipped out. I knew he would keep his word and send me the ticket and papers to follow him to America. I would be a war bride, and why not. There were thousands of us. What did I leave behind? Good jobs were scarce, there was not enough food, and it would take years for things to get better. I had to go through some kind of cultural training, imagine that, it was like an army camp where a group of young girls were brought together, all *Fräulein* from the American occupied zone who were to follow their men to the promised land. Some of them had children already. They trained us not to become soldiers, but perfect American housewives, taught us how to make hamburgers, told us about Thanksgiving and showed us how to put diapers on baby dolls. It was all quite ridiculous. I had no intention of becoming a housewife, I wanted a job, a career, and earn my own money. But I played along and pretended to be grateful for the instructions.

Some of the girls were in for a surprise, I can tell you that. The hero of their dreams, handsome in their uniforms, smashing, actually, often turned out to be coalminers from Kentucky, and very poor. It was most difficult for the girls who had fallen in love with one of the black soldiers. They weren't prepared for the racism and discrimination in some of those southern towns they moved to. Many found out the hard way that the American Dream we all had dreamed of back then after the war wasn't for everybody. But a few of us did get lucky. I did. I had seen Bobby's photographs of his home, and of his mom, and they were real. This was more than a step up for me, from the old three-winged farmhouse with the drafty and smelly outhouse to a two-story house with a bathroom attached to each bedroom, wall-to-wall carpeting and a kitchen like I had never seen in my old village. I didn't mind that we were to live with my mother-in-law. We would be able to save and purchase our own place eventually. I've always been practical about these things. Set your eyes on a goal and work your way towards it. Getting to America, that was my goal.

Some girls faced challenging times, you know. Their boys had trouble adjusting to normal life, and sometimes they took it out on their war brides. The German Foreign Office had special funds ready, in case the girls wanted to return home, if things turned out to be unbearable for them. They just needed to contact the Consulate here, and they made sure you got a ticket home. I wonder how many took advantage of that and had the courage, or experienced the desperation to return to Germany. What happened to them, especially when they had kids? Did they have to leave them behind? They certainly could not play the part of the elegant American when they returned to their old hometowns. How could they.

Life takes strange turns.

I knew this was not going to happen to me. I simply wouldn't let it happen. I was excited about the trip, about seeing Bobby again and meeting his family. It wasn't such an easy journey as it is today, you know. I've always loved traveling, but that first crossing took me a full week to get to Omaha. I had to take a propeller plane to London and then one to Iceland, and from there we crossed the Atlantic to New York, Papa's hometown. We stayed a few days to sort out immigration. I barely had time to see the skyscrapers, the Statue of Liberty from a distance, before I took that little plane to Omaha, the last bit of my long trip. I felt sick for days.

It was only 1947, the War Bride Act had been passed the year before, but wasn't applied to German women, so they had to wait another year. It was finally legal to marry a foreign-born girl and to fraternize with the enemy's daughters. We didn't have much to take with us. During the war we had made clothes out of old army coats and later dresses out of parachute silk, if we were lucky enough to get our hands on it. They made nice cocktail dresses. I was pretty good at trading things on the black market, and I wanted to make sure I would arrive in style, a war bride who didn't look like the others, who knew how to dress and had nice luggage. Whose English was good, without a thick German accent, the enemy's accent. Bobby had left me with generous supplies which I traded for fabrics, and a friend turned them into dresses, a coat, a suit. I was determined to arrive as a sophisticated young lady. I didn't really know what the word meant, but I had heard it used in one of those instructional films they showed us in the prep camp. I wanted to impress my new family.

Was it hard to leave, you ask? Well, to be honest, leaving Mama and Papa wasn't easy, but I never looked back at the village. Papa encouraged me to go. I was worried about Willi, your father, who hadn't come home yet from the prison camp somewhere in Croatia, but there was nothing I could do for him. And I would find work, send packages home, and help Papa, Mama and Willi that way. I decided to look ahead, not back.

I have never been the sentimental kind, you know, not then, and not later when things fell apart, when life seemed dark and hopeless, at least for a while, quite a while ...

When Bobby met me at the airport, I burst into tears, couldn't hold them back because I was so happy and relieved to see him. My mascara was running down my cheeks. I must have looked dreadful. I held on to him and just couldn't let him go. I was so tired after this long trip, but I wanted to look good not just for him but for my new family, too. You, know, first impressions. I asked Bobby to stop at a gas station where I went to the ladies' room to wash my face, brush my hair and reapply some lipstick, the one I had traded for half a pound of coffee. It wasn't really my color, magenta, but it was the only one I could get my hands on. Always wear lipstick, it makes you look fresh.

And then there was Betty, my mother-in-law. I knew she wasn't keen on meeting this *Fräulein* from Germany. But she was kind and so elegant, *sophisticated*. I instantly became her task, she started working on me right way. I felt like Eliza in My Fair Lady. She threw out my carefully traded black market clothes, thought them unsuitable for an American lady and gave them to the salvation army. My teeth, which had suffered from bad food and, yes, poor hygiene, were pulled or capped. My German past was covered by a complete make-over. And I let her do it. From now on I would wear matching shoes and purse. I trusted Betty, and as a practical-minded aspiring American, I played along. I wanted more than anything to blend in. I wanted to be like them, well-fed, worry-free, clean Americans. Antonia became Toni.

It was hard for a while. I wasn't allowed to work, and Omaha wasn't exactly the center of the world. There wasn't much to do, no clubs, really, no dancing, drinking with the boys, so I watched a lot of television, learned the language, studied the American way of life, imitated the gestures and phrases and got quite good at it. But I needed to learn how to write the language, not just speak if I ever wanted to find a job, so I took classes, too. There were other girls from Germany in my language class, but I kept my distance. Germany was the past. I was looking out the front window, not the back. My car was going forward towards a new life. Leave the past in the rear window, forget that your heart aches, that you miss home. And eventually build your own house, with a bay window that faces the woods and a lake in a landscape that looks a little like the Rhine valley.

Bobby–well, he was still Bobby: reckless, a gambler, passionate lover, a devoted son, and not exactly reliable when it came to the more mundane things in life. First he wanted to go back to school. Then he decided he wanted to make money right away. He sold cars for a while, what a job, but he really was a born salesperson, charming and persuasive. He got bored and finally signed up with a big insurance company. He was on the road all the time, often gone for a full week. He needed the free reign, I knew it even back then. And that's where he died, on the road, five years after we got married. Forever young in my memory, the perfect lover, though not the perfect husband. He left me childless.

How ironic that Bobby should die in a car crash caused by that drunk driver. How ironic that he should die because of the recklessness of some drunk who made him swing right on some residential street in Omaha where you wouldn't expect it. Hadn't he been in a war zone? At least that was the official story. There were no skid marks leading to the concrete pillar of an overpass. He received a proper Catholic funeral. I did turn to the church in those dark years, and it brought me consolation. But I couldn't quite forgive him for

Toni (left), Audrey-Hepburn-style

leaving me, and God for not protecting him, deep down in my heart. Why did God allow for him to be taken so early in life?

Why I didn't go home, you ask? That never crossed my mind, even though I missed Mama and Papa. Going back to what? The old farmhouse? The narrowness of village life? I had moved beyond that, had reinvented myself, something that was possible in the new world but not in the old one where stories were told and retold, sins never forgiven. I had become a naturalized citizen in 1951 and was able to provide for myself. I was an

American, an independent woman, modern, stylish on the outside. Inside I had a heart full of holes. Betty was my anchor, she helped me through all this, shared my grief. We made it through this together, really. We bought a new home in town, an even finer house, with washer and dryer, a huge fridge, a porch, something folks at home could only dream of, and a TV cabinet that filled the whole corner in our designated TV room. This new place didn't remind us of Bobby all the time. After a while, we socialized to numb the pain, joined the women's church group. We learned to laugh again.

Until Ted and I decided to get married, but that was much later, almost 30 years later. Ted, my second husband, more a friend, really, a friend for many years. He had seen me at Bobby's funeral. And that's when everything changed for him. He had pitied me, the young widow, loved me, adored me the minute he saw me. Really, it's true, he confessed to me when we finally made plans together for a joint life. Did I need him, and the security he provided? Maybe. He was solid, trustworthy. A rock to stand on. But he was no lover. We began as friends, travelled together, to Niagara Falls, Hawaii, Greece, even to the old village, Papa was very suspicious of him. He didn't understand friendship. But Ted was happy when he could provide for me. Unconditional love, that's what it was. For him, that is. We both retired and left the past behind us, started new here in the Ozarks. Betty came with us, but wasn't happy. She felt too isolated here, but I believe she just couldn't accept my new marriage. So, she left us to be with her daughter. I still miss her. But that's really another story.

Let me sleep a little now in this big old leather chair with Kitty in my lap. When you get old and you can't move around as you used to, make sure you have a cat, something warm, soft and alive. And make sure you have a view. Sister Carrie had a rocking chair, but she had no view. Not even a cat. My mother always had cats, and the cats had babies. Nobody neutered a cat in the village. You took the newborns to the creek and dumped them. You were supposed to do that before they opened their eyes, but sometimes she just waited too long. The poor mama cat searched the whole farmhouse for her babies that the

Toni in Greece, Jackie-O-style

creek leading to the Rhine river had swallowed. You just couldn't keep them all. People in the village weren't sentimental.

My chair faces the bay window. I see the trees, down below dark blue Table Rock Lake, and I watch the hummingbirds. Those beautiful little creatures that look so delicate, but who can be ferocious little fighters. Survivors. They know what they want. And they watch me, too, with their intelligent little eyes. And sometimes, you know, sometimes I can feel Bobby standing behind my chair. Then we talk about those wild days. About passion. I had it once. They never leave us completely, these feelings, and the loved ones.

Let's talk more later.

* * * * *

2013

There are pictures of the house now for sale on the Internet. The rooms are empty, the linoleum floors look shabby without the carpets, the fireplace is cold.

But I still see Toni in her big armchair watching the hummingbirds circle the bird feeder full of sweet red liquid with that spectacular view of Table Rock Lake stretching beneath her patio. I asked Nancy to send the photos Toni had kept, hoping, maybe, for some clues, some insights into that very private life. There is Toni in those happy, reckless years with smashing Bobby, small black-and-white photos from their trips in Germany after the war, their professional wedding pictures, Toni or Bobby posing with the dog. And there are pictures with her mother-in-law at parties, both women elegantly dressed and sparkling with life, Toni looking like Audrey Hepburn, but without Bobby now.

A letter she typed on that thin light blue airmail paper to her family in Germany, but never mailed, is among her papers. It is full of typos and a few grammatical errors, as if she had forgotten her mother tongue. It also suggests that not everything was as exciting in that Nebraska town as she had hoped, especially not after Bobby's death:

Omaha, Sept. 18, 1956

Das Wetter ist jetzt hier sehr schoen. Kuehl abends und morgens und ueber Tage noch ziemlich warm. Naja, man hat ja weiter nicht viel davon. Es ist aber auch zu schade, dass man hier nichts anfangen kann. Es ist nur ein Glueck das man Fernsehen hat und das die Programme gut sind sonst wuesste man garnicht was man fuer Unterhaltung anfangen sollte. E was muss man ja schlieslich haben und alleine wohin gehen wie ins Kino oder so dazu habe ich auch keine Lust. Well, ich weiss sonst eigentlich nichts mehr zu schreiben.

(The weather is very nice now. Cool in the evenings and mornings and still quite warm during the day. O well, one can't really enjoy it much. It is too bad, there is nothing to do here. Lucky that one has television and that the programs are good otherwise one wouldn't know what to do for entertainment. One must have something and to go alone to the cinema or so I don't feel like doing that. Well, I just don't know what else to write.)

There are only a couple photographs from the years Toni shared with Ted in the Ozarks, no wedding pictures, no party photos, no friends. They were both content with each other's company. But then there were these long, twenty years Toni spent alone in her Ozark home, though well provided for: Toni with her books and birds, regular church visits as long as that was physically possible, cherished weekend visits by Nancy with lots of laughs and a glass of champagne, two pralines each filled with liquor, and the occasional phone call–from home.

Had Toni known that the designated caretaker of her beloved cats would declaw them right away, plague them with all possible shots and treatments, and spend a third of the allotment on all that, she would surely have thought of a different solution. Cats without claws–she would have been horrified. She loved wild things.

SEVEN
Do you like Honey?
1980

He sat next to her in the "Introduction to American Literature" class. A good-looking fellow with soft brown eyes and long lashes. He was what she had imagined an American college boy might look like. The outdoorsy type, flannel shirt, jeans, blond hair. He was not very tall, but not small either and walked like a cowboy swaying his hips and bending his knees a bit. After the second or third class, he invited her for a walk across campus.

"Do you like honey?"

Iris was a bit confused. What did he mean? Her mind wasn't able to figure out the obvious.

"I don't like words like that," she replied thinking he was trying to flirt with her. Her English was pretty good—when discussing literary texts in class—yet, everyday English was a different matter. Easy conversations, meaning hidden behind words, smart responses—you did not learn that in school. She instantly realized her mistake and tried to correct it. Iris usually did not blush, but now her face felt hot and red.

She was an American culture brat, loved the ease and the coolness of the actors in her favorite shows. As a kid she had dreamed about Sandy in "Flipper"—also a boy from Florida, tanned, smart, a loving brother and caring son. She watched all the classics, the Western movies with John Wayne, Gary Cooper, Rock Hudson and the likes. She loved musicals and favored the muscular and athletic Gene Kelly over the gaunt, elegant Fred Astaire. She always preferred the strong male Hemingway type, the one who knew what was right, who had learned the hard way and harbored a melancholy which had to be lifted from his heart—preferably by a woman. Total kitsch, of course.

So here he was, her version of Sandy whose image merged with the real boy and made her assume similar qualities as the faultless film version.

This year abroad was supposed to be her big adventure. Iris had always dreamed of living under palm trees, under a sky so blue and sunshine as predictable as the sudden afternoon rainfalls. They passed quickly and left the ground steaming. Nightfall came without warning in this part of the world, no long summer evenings with a blue hour and slowly fading lights. That she missed. She also missed life as an adult student hanging out with friends, talking politics or books through the night, going to the little wine places in her neighborhood at home, wondering if one could afford a second glass of chilled white Riesling and perhaps some cheese. Iris loved those lazy summer evenings.

Here she had descended into college life. She occupied a lovely corner room on the third floor of a stately red brick building with two windows, quite spacious for a student dorm. But her home now was an all-girls dorm, most of them younger by three or four years, lovely American girls, many from well-off families attending this small private college founded by Methodists. Although it was 1980, there were still young women whose mission in college was to find their beaus. The choice of restaurant or bar for your first date was telling, and, of course, the boy was expected to pay. Although some of the young women were going out with boys, they "kept" themselves for *the one*. They confided about the night spent with him, but they would not have sex—at least so they claimed. Looks were crucial, and a lot of time was spent on shaving your legs, plucking your eyebrows and putting those big curlers in your hair to look like Farah Fawcett. Big-hair-girls were sexy.

Though Iris was a small-town girl, she felt this place to be a long way from her German university, and not just geographically. Nobody there cared if you shaved your legs, and you paid for your own glass of wine and cheese dish. One did not read a deeper meaning into the quality of the date based on the choice of restaurant. Though young women and men also dreamed of Mr. and Ms. Perfect, they were a goal to work towards, years into the future. Marriage was unthinkable at that stage of their lives. Living together was a possibility, or better sharing a place—to reduce costs, not out of love. Don't get too serious, finish your studies first, get a career, be independent. And don't talk about love. It might frighten the boy away.

And now this dorm room, where no boys were allowed, would be her home for the next ten months. "Men in the hall," was the standard shout when the plumber would come up to fix the clogged shower drain. The only exception to the No-Men-Rule was the lobby with its big sofas and TV screens, and the open house once a year. Then visitors were allowed—as long as the doors stayed open. Nobody came to visit her that afternoon, although she had hoped *he* would come. Iris was too shy to ask him, but secretly hoped he would surprise her. He was not the surprise kind of guy, and not the courting one either. They would never meet on her turf.

There was something pleasant in this comradery among the girls in her dorm. Together they enjoyed pizza and M&M nights, talks about classes and dates, worried about gaining too much weight and not getting enough exercise. Janette with her little girl's face, long brown curly hair and long legs looked 16 at the most, but was going steady with a boy at home in Arkansas who was waiting for her to finish college. Jeanine, a freckled mature young woman with green catlike eyes, had recently moved from Alaska to Florida with her parents and a younger brother. It must have been a difficult move. Their house, a one-story bungalow to which she had been invited over a long weekend, was sparsely furnished with curtains drawn in front of overstuffed shelves serving as closets and plastic chairs around the dinner table. How they were able to afford college for their eldest remained a mystery, but Jeanine worked hard all summer long in the mall to help with the expenses. Leyla, an elegant Arab-American girl from West Palm Beach, arrived with her whole family in tow who set her up in the dorm room. They brought rugs, pillows and throws to make the place look almost lavish and a little bit like home for their little princess. She was supposed to get married right after college, but this was her precious time away, and she discretely used it well.

Stella, an awkward pale girl with straight black hair, bangs that got in her eyes and a slight hunch, who was proud of her home town Monticello, and, in a strange way, seemed ageless, became her tennis partner. There was nothing else to do on Saturday and Sunday mornings but play tennis on the concrete courts, or walk around the lake. Nobody had a car on her floor to go to the famous Florida beaches Iris had always wanted to see. They were only an hour away, Clearwater Beach, Anna Mariah Island, but as freshwomen they did not know the fraternity boys yet who could have given them a ride. Only at the end of her second term did Iris find out that one of the boys from her history class, a sophomore, had tried to call her several times on Saturday mornings to ask if she wanted to come along to Clearwater Beach. He never left a message and never said anything when they met Tuesdays and Thursdays in "American History I" and "American History II". Iris would have loved it, especially because she liked that kid, a passionate surfer, another "Sandy" but softer and younger, more her brother's age. Only then did they manage to go out, listen to Peter Gabriel's new song "Games Without Frontiers" in his little red car and the live version of Pink Floyd's "The Wall". He would become number one on a list of "we'll-probably-never-see-each-other-again" passionate farewell encounters that were safe and at the same time heartbreaking. Had she not missed those Saturday morning phone calls, who knows how different her exchange year might have become.

But then here was "Sandy", or rather "Rob", as he called himself. His whole family called him Bob, but he decided to try out that new "Rob" persona in college. He lived off campus in his own apartment, had worked for a couple of years to return for his junior year and study towards a degree in business administration.

"I want to become an entrepreneur," he said, a word Iris had to look up in her yellow dictionary which she had left in her room because it was too big to carry around in her handbag. She did not ask him what it meant for fear of looking stupid. So many new words to learn. "Procrastinating" was another that one of the sun bathers explained to her by the pool where she sometimes spent an hour or two in the afternoon. He was wearing the Star of David on a golden chain around his neck, the first Jewish boy, or person, for that matter, she had ever met until then. Talking to him, a nice kid from New York, made her feel intensely German. You never knew what his family had gone through, where they had come from, what tragedy they had had to endure because of the Germans. She felt too insecure to befriend him.

Iris found it strange that Rob wanted to become an entrepreneur. In what? Doing what? Her German friends talked about becoming a teacher or lawyer, working in advertising, something concrete. Her generation still followed their parents' advice, find a life-long employment, do the best you can but play it safe. In America, kids obviously dreamed bigger. It was part of their DNA. Only one of her German university friends, a Philosophy and German major, dared to think big, but more out of necessity. Or desperation? When he could not get into the teacher training program after graduation because there were no openings, he retrained as a computer expert, became self-employed, talked about registering his business at the stock exchange with the goal of retiring at age 45. He didn't succeed. Once he fell asleep on a train, and when he woke up, his laptop was gone with all the business documents he had needed to prepare for this one, great deal that would have changed everything. Or so he claimed. The German system doesn't tolerate failure. In America, you could try things out, fail, start new. You always got a second chance, a third. You just had to take it.

The College campus, as pretty as it was, felt a bit isolated. The town's center was a few miles away, if you could call it that, and public transportation was a vocabulary Americans probably had to look up in a dictionary. The streets leading to the shopping area did not have sidewalks, and nobody walked anywhere unless it was part of your daily exercise. There was a Greyhound station for travel between the cities, but any self-respecting student attending the private college would not take it. Once Iris and Jeanine took a bus to the big mall outside of Tampa, but her friend made sure not to tell her mother about the trip. She would have freaked out about her daughter taking such a risk and mingling with poor folks. You did not want to belong to them, even if your own house was barely furnished and money was tight.

Rob gave her a lift to the store occasionally so she could stock up on little things like shower gel, shampoo and some sweets. He proudly showed her a gas station where you could shop throughout the night. He wondered if she was not afraid of the Russians who were stationed right there on the German border. After all, this was still the Cold War, but to her this was a strange question. Iris did not tell him that they, too, had electric toothbrushes and gas stations where you could shop. At least, he knew more than many other students who had asked her if she was from East Germany.

On election day he continued her introduction to the American way of life. He took Iris to the polling station in his hometown and showed her how the process worked in the land of the free. Rob was a staunch Reaganite while Iris preferred Jimmy Carter whom she had heard speak on a nearby campus. Who would vote for a

B-movie actor, she wondered, but she did not challenge Rob on his political views. She lacked the words, which made her feel stupid because she loved talking about politics. Rob persuaded the poll workers to let her watch him punch the ballot in the voting booth, a system she recalled many years later when it became an issue in the famous Bush/ Gore election of 2000.

That day in November after exercising his right as an American to determine the fate of the future President, Rob took Iris to his parents' house about an hour and a half away from the college town. They owned a spacious, pleasant home surrounded by white fences and backed by stables. He showed her around, quite proud of the picture-perfect, but somehow sterile farm, obviously not a working farm except for the horses. Walking through the tall, dry grass, he picked up an empty snake skin, at least one-and-a-half meters long. Iris was scared of snakes, afraid they might be curled up right next to her feet. Before coming to Florida, she had read that more snake species lived there than anywhere else in the world, and on a drive to Disney World she had seen a long black snake cross the street ten meters in front of the car in astounding speed. "Just my luck," she thought while trying to hide her fear and forcing herself to keep moving. It amused him.

Rob showed her his "baby", a blue Ford Mustang he kept in a garage next to the stables to work on and for the occasional spin. Too precious to keep in the open parking lot in front of his apartment, he changed his beloved baby for a big blue Ford during the week, a boring car, really. Iris had tried to open the window by her seat, but could not find the handle. "It's all electric, automatic", he had said with a grin lowering her window from the driver's seat, feeling slightly superior. It was a strange day. He was clearly trying to impress her, and yet he stressed what kept them apart, not what brought them together. This was all about "things" and not feelings. His parents were nice, but reserved, probably wondered what kind of relationship their son had with this young woman who was shy and quiet, afraid to make mistakes. Rob had been showing her how democracy worked in America and was clearly impressed with himself.

On the way back to college they were both quietly listening to country music. What was it that attracted her to him, what was it she saw in him? How could she detangle the real boy from the TV heroes, the all-American cool kid from the boy driving her through the night? Rob suddenly stopped in the middle of the road, turning off the lights.

"Get out of the car," he said.

Iris hesitated not quite trusting him. What if he left her here in the middle of nowhere? How would she ever get back?

"Come on, get out of the car," he said holding the door open and, as usual, not volunteering an explanation. And so she did.

"Listen."

Save for the noise the crickets made, there was nothing else, no sound, no cars, no planes, no light. Total darkness. Silence. It was a magic moment on that country road when she felt the soft Florida air on her skin and smelled the earthy, swampy landscape. Looking up, her eyes adjusted to the night under a sky lit by thousands and thousands of stars becoming brighter and brighter. This you would not find in Germany. This was special. He was special. But Iris made sure not to set even one foot into the tall grass next to the road.

If this was a story, Iris would have invented him with all his clichés. She liked him, a guy so different from her friends at home. Although the son of a physician, he cultivated the image of the nature guy, the fisherman, outdoor enthusiast, conservative to the bone and proudly American. She loved his body, strong, tanned and muscular, and they soon made love because she hoped to get closer to him, break through that all-American boy image and discover—something. She was lonely, homesick and too aware of being an outsider in that world. A love affair was probably the worst remedy to get over her insecurities.

Iris needed to be back in her dorm by midnight, or she would have to ring a bell to be let in. Then everybody would know she had stayed out so late and gossip would travel the halls. Once she stayed at his place the whole night, sleeping in his arms, feeling safe and secure, but when he dropped her off on campus the next morning, he did not say "Can we see each other tonight?" It was always "See you later," so she kept waiting for him to call. Jeanine, whose room was directly across from hers, caught her in the hallway that morning when she was unlocking her dorm room, so she pretended to have just returned from breakfast. But her clothes gave her away, because she was wearing the same outfit as the night before. Jeanine was discrete, and they never talked about it. Why could they not just be a couple? Iris did not like the secrecy.

Rob's apartment was scrupulously clean, not like her brothers' rooms where clothes from the day before were left in front of the bed and empty soda cans and bags with potato chips on the nightstand for weeks until her mother threw a fit. Rob's walk-in closet housed fishing gear and mysterious gadgets and boxes. He let her stay in his place over Thanksgiving, a long holiday weekend during which her dorm was closed. Her girlfriends invited Iris to come home with them, but she felt uncomfortable as a guest and did not like staying with people she did not know. She wanted to feel independent again, be by herself for a few days, feel like an adult, but also hoped to spend some time with Rob. He had invited her to come to his family dinner, not just out of politeness, but because Thanksgiving was to be shared. To him, being alone over Thanksgiving was as if you spent Christmas alone. Iris declined knowing he had not invited her as his girlfriend and because she couldn't imagine being around his reserved, observing parents again. She pretended she needed the time to work on a term paper for one of her classes. There was always a paper to write. Besides, she would not be completely alone but had some friends who happened to live in his neighborhood, also an older student who shared a flat with his siblings and whose mother taught at the college.

Fred, a tall guy with braces, curly brown hair, freckles and very friendly, was in his mid-twenties. They had both enrolled in "Tennis for Beginners" and become friends. Fred had worked as an airline pilot for several years before going back to college. In Germany, you would not run into somebody like him. Becoming an airline pilot required years of training, and once you landed a job with Lufthansa or so, you definitely stayed in it. It was well paid and glamorous. In spite of his young age, Fred had even flown the big planes. He decided to go back to college to get a Bachelor's degree and then go on to law school. He had it all figured out. What he had not figured out was love. He was in love with one of the girls in her dorm, a sweet blonde first-year student with large blue eyes and beautiful long hair. Big-Farrah-Fawcett-type-hair. She looked like the picture-perfect cheerleader, which made Iris feel clumsy. Fred did not know how to approach her and confided in the German student who seemed so mature. He talked about his Irish-Catholic upbringing and the pressure he felt to live by his parents' strict moral code. He had eleven siblings. A Catholic herself, but the European kind, Iris had a much more liberal view and believed, so she told him, that if you deeply cared for somebody, it was perfectly alright to take the next step. These were the pre-AIDS years which soon would change the game. Fred never mustered the courage to ask Ms. Pretty out, but he got to marry a college sweetheart after all. He did the Catholic thing, married young, probably avoided sex before marriage, became a successful aviation lawyer, and had a couple kids. He seemed happy when she contacted him decades later trying to find a lawyer who could help her with her aunt's estate. A predictable life without too much heartbreak. Why did she never fall for the nice guys? The ones who had it figured out for a change?

For the long Thanksgiving weekend, Iris planned to go over to Fred's on Friday, cook her famous family recipe for spicy onion soup, which was way too hot for a Florida day, and bought a bottle of wine for him, his younger brother Patrick, also a student at the college, and his older sister Mary who worked as a registered nurse and was getting ready for graduate studies in medicine. Iris enjoyed the freedom away from the dorm, and she enjoyed being with the siblings. She should really spend more time with these folks instead of thinking about "Sandy" all the time. She knew that she was letting him determine the rules of the game. With Fred and his siblings, she felt secure, did not worry about making mistakes or looking stupid. This was friendship without heartache.

Not wanting to appear eagerly awaiting Rob's return, Iris made sure his place looked like she wasn't even there. She smelled his flannel shirts and looked for clues in his apartment that would provide a glimpse of the "real" Rob, the one she was determined to discover. When she finally heard his car pulling into the parking space in front of the apartment, she nervously glanced around the room to check if all was in order.

Rob was not in a post-Thanksgiving mood. He complained that Iris had used the wrong towel to dry the dishes and that she had mixed up the central light switch with the switches on the table lamps. He raised his eyebrows when he saw the bottle of wine in the fridge which a friend had sent her from home; annoyed he claimed he did not drink. They had sex, but it was not the gentle loving kind she had hoped for. He had seen his old girlfriend.

For the rest of the term, they saw each other twice a week in class and in Convocation on Wednesdays. Sometimes they passed each other in the common room of her dorm. The girls on her floor warned Iris that they had seen him downstairs and had even figured out who he was waiting for. Iris hesitated a moment upon crossing the hall, heading for an evening jog around the lake with Jeanine. She did not want to let the other girls know how much it bothered her to see him. There he was, sitting in one of the big brown faux leather armchairs watching the news on TV waiting for his date to join him. He looked at her with his beautiful soft brown eyes, but he did not say a thing. She knew the girl he was seeing, and did not think her pretty at all. Would she sleep with him as well? Was *she* looking for a future husband? That evening she completed the four-mile run around the lake for the first time, leaving Jeanine behind who had given up a quarter mile before reaching the frat houses. Rage can do that to you.

Along with the holiday season came the end of the first semester. Her mother had sold her car, an old VW Beetle, so Iris was able to afford a plane ticket to go home for Christmas. Now she would not have a car when she got home, but she knew she needed to be with her folks and friends to feel grounded again. The trip was endless, with a long eight-hour layover at Kennedy airport in New York. Iris was full of regret and hurt feelings which showed as a rash on her face. She had not been able to tell Rob how she felt, had lacked the words, could not even tell him off. Iris was too polite to swear at him in her own language, so the words remained inside, and choked her up. Because of him, that first semester had been a lonely and confusing one. She would make this mistake again, get hung up on a boy or a man craving love and friendship that they were not able to give and, foolishly, let that ruin the precious time she was having in a different world away from home.

When Iris returned to campus at the beginning of the New Year, the weather was grey and wet in her hometown, but not in the sunshine state. There were a few cold nights when the college kids were finally able to get out their warm sweaters, down vests and pretend winter was upon them. The citrus farmers positioned large Bunsen burners around their precious trees and bushes to keep the almost ripe oranges and pink grapefruit from freezing. By all appearances, you could not tell that the inside of the fruit was already dried up, like an empty balloon. Decades later, a colleague who had grown up in the region told her that since then most citrus plantations in Florida have been destroyed by a virus. The air would never smell the way it had back then, with that light, citrus aroma in the dark, balmy Florida night.

Iris hardly saw Rob during her second semester. She was relieved they did not have any classes together. But Wednesdays began, again, with "Convocation", a strange ritual going back to the religious roots of the college during which the whole community assembled in the big theater auditorium to listen to an "inspirational" lecture by their alumni—among them former beauty queens, clergymen, entertainers or politicians. She would see Rob sitting in a seat a few rows in front of her because students were seated in alphabetical order—he in "D", her in "K." Older students checked the rows of assigned seats and kept a list of who had been skipping Convocation. Rob sometimes did. When they ran into each other, they would smile and nod, and go their ways. And she pretended not to care.

Iris befriended an Italian-American graduate student who came twice a week from his university in Tampa, to teach Italian to music students. She enrolled in the class because she needed two more credit points to be a full-time student and had always wanted to learn the language. Alex was European to her, sophisticated, slick, a Latin lover, with thick black hair which he pushed back from his forehead with elegance and ease. He was somebody to have an affair with, not a "Sandy" type to fall in love with at all. He was safe. An easy talker, he paid her compliments and invited her for the weekend to the city an hour away and close to the beach. He cooked pasta with not enough sauce, Italian style, and took her dancing to a discotheque. Though he said all the right things, called quite often and did not keep her waiting till midnight, like Rob, she did not trust him. Alex, too, had a girlfriend in Boston whom he expected for a visit any day now and talked to on the phone even in her presence, which made her feel uncomfortable. He stressed how much money he had to spend on calling her and his girlfriend and that his father's allowance would not leave him much spending money. This friendship became quite complicated and a bit of a nuisance, but at least it did not leave heartbreak and scars. Whenever Iris saw Rob on campus, her heart skipped a beat and the look of his eyes almost made her forgive him for his back and forth, the power game he had been playing with her.

The exchange year came slowly to an end. Iris had enjoyed her classes, felt noticed and encouraged by her professors and received very good grades. They hugged her and asked her to stay in touch. Almost comically, her English professor introduced her to his nerdy son hoping the two of them might become an item. It was instantly clear neither of them was interested. Iris did have one more adventure planned to conclude her exchange year: a trip out west. She could not wait to leave that isolated college town and discover the vastness of the American landscape. A landscape she had admired for years, ever since a kid, watching all those Western movies.

So Iris met up with another exchange student from her university whom she had met briefly before they all had left for their year abroad. Susanne, a blond girl with porcelain skin, came from a wealthy family and used her exchange year to explore a very different life. Her boyfriend, a tall, gangly guy who studied on and off and supported himself through odd jobs, certainly would not have had a chance with her in Germany. Here, Susanne was free to do what she liked and spend time with whomever she liked. She cherished this freedom, the freedom to sleep with a guy she would not have to explain at home, who tried to please but was clearly not in her league—academically nor financially. She met the odd couple at the Greyhound station in Mobile, Alabama, and together they drove to Mississippi where Susanne had spent her academic year. This was not Florida, the groomed campus full of well-off kids with bright futures and dad's credit card.

Leaving Florida; off to the West

165

This was a place one needed to leave behind in order to realize one's dreams, a place to start from, but to get out quickly—and nothing more.

Richard not only borrowed money from his ex-girlfriend, he also borrowed her little red Toyota for the trip—which suggested he would never make it out of town on his own. The three of them were off, heading towards New Orleans, San José, Albuquerque, the Grand Canyon, Mesa Verde, Las Vegas, Death Valley, and finally San Francisco. Iris experienced a deep loneliness traveling with a couple who demonstrated their love life quite openly. Yet she was overwhelmed, and she enjoyed the magnificence of the country, the big sky, the western landscapes, Highway 66 and the surfer boys in California. Pitching her own little tent and talking to fellow travelers she met in various state parks, she, actually, felt strong and confident. When a sandstorm hit in White Sands, they all had to cram into one tent, as, of all places, they had found themselves at the atomic bomb testing grounds abandoned decades ago. They huddled together, much to Richard's delight, who secretly kept a gun under his pillow to protect his two girls—just in case. Other campers grinned about the trio comparing them to "Three's Company," a popular TV show at the time.

Things did not stay free and easy, and, in fact, got quite complicated. Richard left his wallet with his ex-girlfriend's money on top of the girlfriend's red Toyota, while pulling out of the parking lot of a tourist's version of a Scandinavian village, somewhere in California. He only noticed it much later, when they pitched their tents in a state park hours away. He and Susanne retraced their route, hoping an honest person had found and returned the wallet to the lost and found office. For hours Iris waited for them to return. When they finally did return, drunk and giddy on cheap, sweet Gallo wine to soothe their worries, she was relieved to see them. That night, Richard tried to make out with her, to restore his own self-respect, but she did not want to ruin their threesome trip and felt loyal towards Susanne, who now had to cover all his expenses. It did not bother him being dependent, nor did it reduce his appetite for hamburgers and beer, while seeking emotional support from the other fellow traveler. It was time to leave the happy couple in mid-trip.

Iris purchased a Greyhound ticket in San Francisco, which dangerously reduced her funds, to seek refuge with her aunt in Missouri. Two days and two nights on a Greyhound bus brought her in touch with an America she had not encountered before. Strange people befriended her, told her their life story, and vanished again: the private investigator whose grandmother owned a villa in Tuscany, who had been stationed in her German university town and promised to visit on his next trip to Europe; the young ex-convict on his way home from prison to a girlfriend who, in the meantime, had had his baby, yet, he did not know if she would welcome him. He was so moved by their nightly talk that he was reluctant to get off the bus at his stop in the middle of nowhere and expressed his wish to visit Germany one day. He felt people from there seemed so friendly. And then the young man who explained the different cow breeds to her, the Holsteins and Haffers they were seeing while driving by the vast fields. Eventually he talked about his girlfriend who had accused him of molesting her child. Two black women sitting behind them could not believe the stories Iris was told throughout the night. They commented on them with great humor at first, listened attentively and suspiciously after a while, watching over her, the young exchange student from Germany, traveling all on her own. There it was again, the comradery of women. The bus drivers on that long trip also made sure she was alright.

Now Iris had seen more of this vast and beautiful country than Rob. Now she could tell him all about it, which she did upon returning one last time to the perfect Florida college campus with its palm trees, manicured lawns made up of hard, heat resistant leaves and the ever modern Frank Lloyd Wright lecture halls. She stayed with him for one night, knowing it would be their last, secretly and foolishly hoping it would not have to be. Rob was glad to see her, at first, enjoyed her stories and her company, or so it seemed for a while. He, too, knew this had no future, that she was going home. He did not want to talk about what they had shared over these past months and once again pulled back.

The next morning he took Iris to her friends' house where she was to stay for a couple days before leaving for home. They had not spoken since he had woken her up in the night when she had been crying out in her sleep. Iris did not seize that moment of care, the sudden openness. They had had sex without love. He had been cold and careless. She had felt it and could not forgive him. She slammed the car door and left. Words were not necessary any more.

* * * * *

May 2014

e-mail: Trying to contact Ms. K. Please have her e-mail me. thank you

I received your e-mail via our general mailbox. How can I help?

John Wayne from College just wanted to say „Hello"

It's been—what—about 33 years. Pretty amazing . . . Still a John Wayne Fan? What have you been up to? Professionally, in your private life? And what brought this about?

I never have forgotten you and previous attempts to contact you by computer have failed. The computer and the Internet for easy and free communications, international that is, are relatively new to me. But I kept trying.

Iris recognized the name immediately when the webmaster at work forwarded this first e-mail. But somehow the conversation felt odd. She could not put her finger on it, but when he claimed that writing was hard for him, the internet new and that he preferred to talk on the phone, she hesitated. Who knew what had become of Rob. Apparently, he had tried several business ventures that all failed, his kids were in college, his parents' farm sold, and he, semi-retired, was cruising his wife's home state Alabama with his motorbike trying to "still fight the Civil War". This was clearly leading nowhere, and she knew one thing for sure: She did not want to know what he looked like now, her "Sandy", the pretty Florida boy she had loved for a difficult, yet magical year that had determined the course of her professional life. And now all the memories were coming back.

What had she felt? Satisfaction. He had reached out, never forgotten her, a woman now in her fifties mostly invisible to the male world. After all those years.

Not that it mattered—in the big picture. Yet, somehow it seemed as if a fault in a knitting pattern had been corrected, one that had disturbed the rest of that pattern. You could hardly see it anymore. All the rows and loops following looked just right. Something had been put right.

"Go back to your life," Iris wrote.

EIGHT
When Everything Changed
1989

"Your friend Jan called. There is something going on at the border."

"What border, the Hungarian?"

Iris took off her coat thinking of the pictures she had seen on the news of Hungarian border patrols cutting the wire fence and letting East Germans through only a few months before.

"He said you should turn on the TV."

Daniel went back to the kitchen where he was preparing dinner. Small red potatoes cooked in their skin, some veggies and roasted chicken breast now all combined in a cast iron pan and sprinkled with herbs and cheese. He was a good cook, had lived on his own for a long time and enjoyed a fresh home cooked meal. They took turns doing the cooking or the dishes. Both of them were graduate students working on their dissertations. When they had first moved in together a little less than a year after they had met through a mutual friend at the university, they both had felt they had found a partner who could relate to their plight of working on their academic credentials. But lately tensions seemed to have increased.

Iris was sorry to have missed Jan's call, a close friend from school days, with whom she had kept in touch over the years. Yet, to call him back, long-distance, was too expensive. She called her mother once a week, right at six each Monday when it was cheaper, being midnight there. Sometimes her mother was so tired, had even fallen asleep on the couch, but to both it was important to talk, stay in touch. She could not afford any extra calls to Germany. Jan had studied to become a teacher, was now married and teaching full time as a civil servant, receiving a more than decent salary. Unlike her. Iris was not married, nor did she have a well-paying job. She had to carry several jobs, as none alone paid enough to cover her expenses, which, overall, were modest. Except for a plane ticket home once a year, books and a few clothes she enjoyed buying, she was very careful with what she could spend.

Iris was teaching intensive essay-writing classes for the English Composition Board, a central hub at the University that assessed entrance essays and placed the more or less gifted students in the respective writing classes—remedial, regular, advanced, and some even placed out and did not have to take another composition class. She taught the "remedial" classes, which were not called that, only among the students, which entailed three hours of instructions per week plus half an hour of individual consultations. After seven weeks, students had to retake the essay exam, which was again assessed and resulted in placement or out-placement. It was a time-consuming process, but her department was a leading institution in the university's endeavor to increase the quality of writing throughout the curriculum and the disciplines. It took much convincing, the first week, to prove that this course would propel them along, and that, in fact, it was to their advantage to get so much individual attention by their instructors. Iris had excellent colleagues, some experienced writing professionals and a number of gifted graduate students that inspired her. But it was a demanding job. In addition, Iris tutored the college football players, who had to show up at study table several times a week, and this after their long days of classes and daily practice. She could see how tired the young men were. She also worked as a writing tutor at the university's prized business school. While the football players were undergraduates, on a scholarship, with a tough training schedule who also had to fulfill the university's academic requirements, the business school students were working on their MBAs. They had often returned to the university after working for a few years, paid a great deal of money for their education, expecting to land well-paying jobs afterwards. The degree was their ticket to the business world. And the difference between the two groups could not have been more apparent.

All this work allowed Iris only one full day at home, as well as the weekends, to work on her dissertation in American literature. Daniel had a job as an editor for the Middle English Dictionary, 20 hours per week, in which he now worked on entries starting with the letter "n" at a leisurely pace, a term like "nuisance" that was actually derived from old French and meant "injury" or "hurt". She would never have had the patience or mind for such work, but Daniel was a meticulous linguist, and the job suited him. It was not, however, a fulfilling job, as he felt under constant pressure to make progress on his dissertation. Which he did not; but she did, at a laborious, yet even pace. Her progress started to annoy him, because he felt smarter than her, more experienced and better trained as he had been going through a rigorous academic training at first class American universities. Yet, both knew this was not so much about brains and academic training, which they both had, but about "getting it done." Tenaciousness.

"You know what, I managed to write five pages today and expanded on that theory I found the other day in the secondary literature in reference to the *Bildungsroman*," Iris chatted excitedly over dinner after an intensive writing day at her desk at home.

"Great," Daniel mumbled and continued to pick on his food. She missed the signs completely. She was not showing off or trying to make him feel bad, she just longed to share what she was thinking and feeling, hoping for reassurance that she was on the right track. Iris had done the major part of the research and poured her ideas into the keyboard, writing and rewriting. She was somewhat used to this process as a writing instructor. She kept telling her students that rewriting was a must. Nobody was such a genius to write the perfect sentence or paragraph spontaneously. Which was exactly Daniel's problem. He expected to write the perfect sentence, and since he could not, he did not write at all. He got stuck in the bibliography or the projected titles of his chapters while, in fact, he needed to write his prospectus. He did all sorts of things in procrastinating: sharpen pencils, do extensive research in trying to find the perfect desk chair for months, visiting office furniture stores to try out the chairs; learn computer programs on his new MAC, trying to dive deep into coded language. One thing he did not do: make progress on his dissertation.

Daniel had set the kitchen table for dinner. They hardly ate at the large wooden dining set he had brought from his parents' home years ago, loaned out to an ex-girlfriend because his apartment had been too small, and retrieved from her when he and Iris had moved in together. He was trying to keep it in good condition, though he could not fully repair the water stains and traces of ironing because the ex-girlfriend had not exactly returned the precious furniture in mint condition. Daniel had never complained to the previous temporary owner about it. They used the dining set only when they had friends over for dinner, or for the annual Easter brunch. She loved Easter because it was usually the beginning of spring. After a heavy rain everything seemed to turn green overnight in that part of the world. At one of those occasions, quite unintentionally, Iris hit the edge of the table with a pot while serving, which angered him. Upset and hurt by these double standards, she stared him down with the pot in her hands: "One more word, and I'll bang the whole pot into your damn table," she hissed. That had been a clear low point.

The kitchen table was hers, one of the few pieces of furniture she owned in the apartment since she could not bring anything from home. Iris had received it as payment for helping a friend translate a Dutch text for a book project. Though she did not speak Dutch, her mother knew low German, a close dialect she had heard her speak on occasion, the language being a mix of English and German anyway. As a result, she was able to help make sense of the article which he needed for his research on "The History of the Bedroom," a booklet he was writing for a furniture chain. Why the Dutch seemed to know more about the subject escaped her, but they ended up with a kitchen table in their new joint apartment. Ironically, their friend had written his dissertation, then on a typewriter, on this very table and therefore felt nostalgic about parting with it. It seemed wherever one turned, everything was about dissertations these days.

Her own research and writing project was going OK. After her undergraduate year at the college in Florida, Iris had returned to her German university to complete her Master's studies. The year had paid off, the instructors finally had known who she was and that she had had the stamina to invest in a year abroad. Not everybody was ready to do that, leave a boyfriend behind, family and all that was familiar. Since her relationship with Jan had been on-again, off-again for several years, they had simply picked up where they had left off before she had left for the sunshine state. During an off-again phase of that relationship, which had been particularly painful because this time Jan had claimed to have found the woman of his dreams, Iris had often studied the exchange programs posted on the noticeboard outside of the library. Instead of falling into deep depression, she had settled for deep sadness and action: She had registered for the final exams, applied for the teaching exchange and finished her thesis. A month after the oral exams she had found herself completely exhausted in Michigan with two heavy suitcases full of clothes for all seasons and a down coat for the winter. Her brother had given her a brand-new Walkman with extra mini-speakers so she could at least listen to her favorite tapes. Everything else had to be left at home.

The Michigan adventure

Iris had taken over the apartment from the previous exchange student which was conveniently located five minutes away from campus. The house, a historic landmark with a typical wooden porch, was being dwarfed by a student apartment building on the left and a huge concrete carpark with three park decks on the right of the small street. The nights had been noisy, full of constantly partying undergraduate students. The furniture had been old; yet, after a deep clean and adding a colorful throw, some nice pillows, fresh flowers and plenty of new books, she had felt quite comfortable. It was the first time she had been living on her own, and she had liked it. She had explored the small college town, found a Jewish Deli that sold real cheese and good bread, a liquor store that sold wine from her region, and she had settled in.

Iris had been anxious about teaching, but luckily she had had some experience teaching adult students in night school at home. In addition to a class in "Intro Comp", she picked up a teaching job with the "Great Books Honors' Program" in her first semester, which usually assembled a cast of bright graduate students from various disciplines as teaching assistants around the charismatic classics professor. The fact that she was German had appealed to some of the Philosophy majors, who constantly quoted Hegel and Nietzsche, neither of whom she had ever read, and overrated the German academic system. But Iris had found her tribe. If all of these folks were working on their dissertations experiencing numerous challenges and overcoming anxiety attacks, then so could she. In Germany, she would have been a very lonely graduate student with most of her friends having left the university after the Master's program and no graduate schools available to her. Here she had made friends quickly.

One year had been too short to decide which direction her thesis or the relationship with Daniel should take. As a result, Iris had found a way to line up another teaching job with the English Composition Board, as well as some tutoring jobs, which allowed her to renew her visa. Before heading home for part of the summer, they had driven down to Missouri where Daniel had dropped her off at her Aunt Toni's house in the Ozarks on his way to see his family. Iris had then visited her family in Germany to break the news to them that she was not coming back. She had met with her dissertation advisor to plan the next steps, and returned to Michigan to reunite with Daniel. The future had looked bright.

Back in the university town, they had gone apartment hunting and eventually found a two-bedroom apartment up on Summit Hill. Daniel knew the neighborhood which had been a mixed one, early on, and thus not too expensive. He had lived a few streets down at the edge of the summit with other graduate students for a year or two in an old brick house with gables and surrounded by tall pine trees. The house had a lovely view overlooking some fields and parts of downtown. It was probably a dump inside from all the generations of students who kept moving in and out annually. Yet, her fantasy was that it had been a family home, at some point, an old house with a solid structure and character and the potential for a better future. If only they could have moved into a place like that, she thought and renovated it in her mind.

Theirs became a duplex with aluminum siding, cheaply built, but clean and with a lot of light. Upstairs lived the new owners, Paul and Pam Merica, a young couple expecting their first child. *Merica*, how ironic their last name. They were hard-working people living in an adult world. Paul, round-faced and good-natured, had his own business, could repair anything and fixed up the place for his soon-to-be family. Pam, a dark-haired tall woman made pretty with the extra pounds of early pregnancy, worked until days before she was due. They would soon move out again, but not soon enough for the renters downstairs who were kept up by the baby wailing day and night though the thin floors and walls. The Mericas moved on to the next cheap house to fix it up while renting out the old place, firmly on their path to solid middle class. This before the subprime mortgage scams put a stop to upward mobility. Daniel looked at them with some honest admiration, yet also with a bit of contempt. Here he was, the same age as Paul, but nothing to show for but a graduate degree in

Medieval English Studies and struggling with his dissertation. His own father, at that age, had been in the war as part of a mountain battalion stationed somewhere in Finland, had returned to St. Louis to go to law school, and, eventually, built up his own law firm. Daniel could just see his white-uniformed father skiing in a chain of soldiers down a Finnish mountainside close to the Russian border, a rifle tied to his back in their hunt for Nazis. But maybe he got that image from a James Bond movie.

His dad had gotten married at 34, to a lovely wife with whom he had four children within the next ten years. He, too, had moved the family from one house to the next, from an average middle-class area to an affluent neighborhood and a stately home several mortgages above the Merica's. He had realized only too late that work was not everything, as his wife died before the youngest was even in college. Her death had left the family desolate, without a center and him with a bitterness he tried to subdue, which made him constantly irritable. Being the one always to take charge, the widower had remarried within a year in the hopes of restoring that family center. He had married another lovely woman, his total opposite, an artist and dreamer who loved his children, was also widowed, and with two of her own, yet could not ever replace their mother. The family house was sold, the extra furniture stored in a barn at the new wife's farm outside of the city. When Daniel visited, he went through the old stuff and brought a few items for the new apartment that he had moved into with his new girlfriend.

They shared a study with their desks made of planks, on top of two fruit boxes facing opposite walls. Daniel owned the only computer, a much cherished MAC, which Iris used to type her dissertation, as well, when he did not need access. Iris made sure not to disturb the neatly lined up and sharpened no. 2 pencils; the leather tray for coins and paper clips; and the photo of the family before his mother's death. Daniel loved solid things, quality workmanship and timeless designs, things like his classic desk chair made of wood, in which he swiveled back and forth, while thinking about what else to do before opening that intimidating document, the bibliography he kept combing through, refining and adding titles he meant to check out or look up in the library, yet one more time.

In addition to the study, they had a large kitchen, a living room and a small bedroom. At least they did not face a parking lot or student dorms, but hedges of lilacs around their unkempt backyard and tree-lined streets. They had a large painting on loan from an artist friend and framed Danish designer fabric with abstract black paint brush strokes on brilliant white to make the place look less conventional.

"Are we hanging Joan's painting upside down?", Iris asked while Daniel was sliding the painting onto one of the two nails he had placed on either side while she was trying to do the same on her side. There was no way to tell, so they closely examined in what direction the paint had been dripping along the canvas. They had hung the painting upside down. Next time Joan, the artist, visited, she was generous but admitted it when pressed. Joan emphasized the temporary owner's right to hang it any way they liked, so they had left it. Iris could never figure out what the painting was supposed to express, but sometimes the red abstract figure in the center felt outright angry.

The new living arrangement had asked for an unspoilt mattress, so Daniel had researched futon beds, which also looked cool, and they had finally, after many store visits, purchased one. His research had not revealed that a futon tended to be quite firm, so after a few months, lots of back pain and sleepless nights they had sold it and bought a boring boxspring bed. The bedroom looked less cool, but it was comfortable. On her belly with a pillow under her arms Iris would regularly spend an hour watching "Star Trek The Next Generation" after dinner which aired several times a week. The crew always managed to get out of the most difficult situations under the steady guidance of Captain Picard. The show kept her sane in times of too much teaching, writing, and a relationship that was going nowhere. Never again did she watch any show with such intensity. She did not hear the phone nor anything else. For an hour each evening, Iris was totally lost in space.

"Why don't we buy a couch so we can watch TV in the living room," she had asked Daniel several times. The bedroom had turned more and more into a television room, a danger to one's sex life, clearly. "We don't even have a single comfortable chair. I'm sure we could find a couch either second hand or new, and not too expensive."

"Oh, I don't know," he would answer squirming in the director's chair of which they had purchased two to complement the kitchen table. "We'll move again for certain once we're done with the dissertation, and we would have to schlepp all that stuff across the country. Who knows where we are getting jobs—if we're getting any …," he answered moodily. Indeed, when would that be, she wondered. Repeated efforts of persuasion made it very clear to her that Daniel would buy kitchen chairs and a bed because you just needed those, but everything else was to be put on hold, like discussions about their future.

Everything in their lives was temporary, the jobs they had, the apartment they lived in, even the town or the country. Possibly the relationship, too. It was not so much a dream deferred, but an uncertain promise to a better place, a good college or university job in an attractive town God knew where, a decent salary that made up for the stinginess of their endless student years. Every year their group of friends shrunk as some of them finished their degree. They took jobs all over the country, some better than others, while everybody else was still toiling along, meeting on Fridays for happy hour over a pitcher of beer or Margaritas. The job market was a constant topic.

Jason, a tall guy fancying himself descended from ranchers out west with a prominent Buffalo-Bill-style mustache and polished snake-skin cowboy boots, could not hide his gleeful smile when he announced his contract with the University of Texas, tenure-track. He had landed that job with a dissertation written determinedly in barely three years on the Sex Pistols because the English Department put a new emphasis on popular culture. It had been a gamble which had paid off. It was a niche he fit perfectly to everybody's envy. Others, bright young scholars working on Shakespeare, Milton, Emily Dickinson or Robert Frost, feared that they would have to take jobs with four-year colleges somewhere in the midwestern desert, that's how desperate they felt when Jason announced his triumph, with a two-year contract for 18,000, maybe 22,000 a year if they were lucky. And they still had to pay off their student loans. Some never finished, still wrote job applications filling in "ABD", an abbreviation for "all-but-dissertation" pretending they were still at it. Many began to regret that they had not studied law or gone to business school, but it was a bit late for that.

Daniel was better off than most of them. No student loans because dad, the successful lawyer, had invested wisely and set up a trust fund for his four children to get them started in life. A monthly allowance covered living expenses, and the rest came from the MED job. And yet, he was probably the most miserable of the whole lot, though it did not show. To them he was handsome, bright Daniel, respected in his job, yes, struggling a bit with his dissertation, but weren't they all, a man women were attracted to instantly. And now he lived with that graduate student from Germany and was talking about going abroad.

Daniel's biggest obstacle, though, was buried deep inside him, his quiet suffering that he could never please his father. Iris knew that, but she could not help him, though she tried. He sometimes teased her about being like his father when she determinedly took on another teaching job to make sure she would get her visa renewed while still plodding along with her academic work. He called it the German in her. She was never sure if it was meant as a compliment, probably a reflection of his admiration for his father which easily turned into intimidation.

Daniel, thirty already, though looking younger, athletic, casually but well dressed, round glasses, blond, was just her type, she thought, and turned around to look after him every morning they separated on campus and walked to their respective offices in opposite directions. She loved looking at him. He probably didn't know because he never turned around. But there was also something a bit awkward, insecure in his walk, a hesitation and a stiffness, his toes slightly moving inward. With the torso of a swimmer, he looked like he belonged in the water, where he was graceful, and not on earth, where he functioned, but never loosened up like in the water. Maybe his lovers had sensed that vulnerability, which attracted them, but which made him erode every relationship, slowly until they, or he, realized they could not help him. Iris had run into several other ex-love interests among the graduate students, attractive and bright women. When one of her friends had heard about their plans to move in together, she had expressed doubts to her, wondering if Daniel was really ready to settle down. "What does she know about our relationship," Iris had wondered back then. Finally she had a boyfriend who was telling his friends and family excitedly about her, that he had met "this woman from Germany," then that they were moving in together, finally that he was thinking about going to Germany, spend a year on that exchange program with one of the two German universities the department had, the one she had been on.

How great it would be trying out living with him in Germany for a year, Iris had thought, hopeful that this was indeed his plan. She had always been a bit homesick, only relaxed after she had booked her flight home for the summer early in the year to get a good price, had that departure date in mind throughout the spring, something to look forward to. It was no coincidence that she was investigating the "concept of home" in one of her chapters and dealt with a writer who had been to Germany repeatedly and written some chapters set there in his novels. She lived in both worlds, enjoyed being part of the academic community here, profited immensely from it, more than she could ever have in Germany, and yet she missed the landscape, the language, family and friends.

It had been Daniel's plan, all his idea, to apply for the fellowship; she did not have to talk him into it at all. But first he needed to finish his prospectus, then he wanted to make more progress on his writing. He had finally applied in the spring four years into the relationship, not to her home university, which would have been so much easier, but the other alternative two hours north of her hometown. He had not wanted to be close to her family. But it had been too late. The train had left the station. He had not been chosen, because they had picked a younger graduate student, not him who had been in his sixth year of graduate work. He had felt the sting, the rejection.

Daniel had called Iris in the office to let her know that he had been turned down. It had probably been easier than facing her at the kitchen table over dinner. All she could say was: "OK." The whole much discussed and delayed application process had been a disappointment, still was, but she had seen it coming. It was also the end of a dream. Iris was the one making the commitment to this relationship by returning, again and again, to the university and their joint life after the summer. Daniel had visited her twice in Germany, but it had always been a difficult time because she had been trying to please everybody. She had to be a constant translator, not just of language, but also culture, family culture. They could not travel much because money was tight. The first time they had visited the Black Forrest using her dad's car. But when the room they had rented in a little bed-and-breakfast had cost 20 Marks per person per night, and not per room, they had had to cut that trip short.

"If Daniel had gotten the fellowship, would things have turned out differently?", Iris wondered putting her books and the stack of student papers she had to grade on her desk. She had noticed that she put off coming home, stayed in the office longer, walked rather than take the bus. Too often it was coming home to a moody place. Where had the fun, the laughter gone? The banter, warmth, the sex, the gin tonics out on the stairs in the afternoon while listening to "All Things Considered" with Deidre Berger reporting from Berlin, and Garrison Keillor's monologue on "Prairie Home Companion"?

Whatever Jan had wanted her to know about could probably wait, so Iris joined Daniel in the kitchen. She poured a glass of water and a glass of wine for herself and opened a beer for him. He did not like drinking beer out of a glass, preferred the bottle claiming it tasted better. She didn't like that, but accepted it. They had dinner, she told him about her day, and he was pleasant enough.

"I better go and check out the news," Iris said after she had cleaned the dishes because it had been her turn. "Wanna come?"

But Daniel was reading the paper in the living room, a passion they usually shared. Both spent hours reading the New York Times on Sundays, which gave you black fingers, and a wealth of interesting stories, book reviews and international news. They had so much in common, loved books and movies, enjoyed the company of their friends. But they left a lot unsaid. They never seriously talked about the future. Iris did not even know if he wanted kids, which was OK at the moment, because that would have meant making a final decision of where they would live, that she would stay in America most likely. Daniel loved his little nephews, one and three years old, whom they had visited a couple times, first in New York, then in Minneapolis where the family had moved. Iris looked at the kids and wondered if hers would be as cute. They could have easily been Daniel's kids, looked just like him. In many ways, she and Daniel complemented each other. It was little things that annoyed her. He was neat, liked a clean apartment, but most of the work fell on her, although Iris had three jobs. He never made the bed, which she could not stand, but she did not complain because she hated to fight. She loved to slip under the well-shaken duvet and straightened, cool sheets. But these days, in fact for quite a while, they had been slipping under the cover to sleep, turning away from each other facing the opposite wall. When she had the courage to ask him why that was, afraid of his answer, he said: "I'm going through this phase. You feel more like my sister at the moment, and I wouldn't sleep with her either."

Iris turned on the television and settled, belly down, on her side of the bed with her big fluffy down pillow she had brought from Germany under her arms. Crowds were celebrating what looked like New Year's Eve in the streets, champagne glasses and beer bottles in their hands. But it was only November. People were climbing on top of a wall waving flags, German flags, as Peter Jennings was trying to explain over the noise what was going on. Not *a* wall, THE WALL! Berliners welcoming stunned East-Berliners, joined in delirious joy for the first time in four decades. People lifting total strangers up to stand on that damn wall, others chipping off parts, swinging hammers and chisels. Little funny looking East-German cars crossing into the West, being welcomed as never before, and never after, by enthusiastic, teared-up folks. And here she was, almost 7,000 kilometers away in a university town in Michigan.

Only three months before on his second visit to Germany, Iris and Daniel had both hitched a ride to Berlin and stayed in a friend's apartment in Kreuzberg, the then eastern part of West Berlin, the divided city, a first for both of them. It had been an emotional visit for her. When passing Weimar, thinking of the rich history of the town, Iris had shuddered upon seeing the tower of the KZ Buchenwald in the distance. She had asked herself how it was possible to divide a country and a culture, and regretted that they could not simply take a little detour, leave the transit route and explore the part of Germany that had been cut off, closed off, to casual visitors. Of course, this was strictly forbidden. They only had had permission to transit to West Berlin, and driven on. They had explored East Berlin, crossed via Friedrichstrasse train station under the intimidating stares of the young border policemen. They had walked through what would become the fashionable, back then the dreary, colorless "Mitte" district. In amazement, they had looked at the ruins of the burnt-out Synagogue on Oranienburgerstrasse, and, exhausted, they had ordered *Rotkäppchensekt*, a GDR bubbly, at a local pub.

Wherever they had gone, they had stuck out, had spoken English, looked Western. Iris had tried to keep conversations low. From Alexanderplatz, that drafty, empty square surrounded by a few department stores and socialist architecture, they had hiked to the once stately, and partly reconstructed, avenue Unter den Linden. Standing in front of the impressive main building of Humboldt University, Iris had wondered to herself: "Wouldn't it be nice to teach here one day?" After dinner at a restaurant in the Nikolai district, the heart of the original village of Berlin on Fishers' Island, which had been recently rebuilt for the 750th anniversary of the city, they had bought a few books, which had been cheaper than in the West. They had been instructed to spend their GDR money, an *obligatory minimum exchange* per visit, before crossing back into the western part of town before midnight. It had been the reverse of the Cinderella story: you crossed back from a fascinating, yet somehow unreal closed-off eastern part of the city to the glittering West. Their Kreuzberg neighborhood, however, in some ways had resembled the East. Their apartment's toilet had been partitioned off from the kitchen, but did not even have a sink, let alone a shower. They had to wash in the kitchen where the sink was piled up high with dirty dishes the other apartment residents had left there. Iris had hated that place. The glitter was more in the fashionable Kudamm part of town with the expensive department stores and designer boutiques she loved to stroll by. Window-shopping was her great luxury.

They had hastened back to the Friedrichstrasse station with its underground stalls shortly before midnight through which they were to return to the West. Iris had scolded Daniel who had held on to a few of the light, tinny coins as a souvenir. He had not been concerned at all, not about being identified as an American, nor about taking some of these cheap coins back which had been strictly forbidden. He did not have that fear in him that most Germans shared: a deep-seated suspicion of authority, the military, of conflict. Nobody had stopped them, and Iris had felt foolish.

The next day they had hiked along the wall on the western side, which cut off neighborhoods, dividing friends and families, a foreign, frightening object that was meant to be there for at least the next hundred years, as East German leader Erich Honecker had declared only in January 1989. To make it less menacing, artists had covered the western side of the wall with murals and graffiti while the wall on the eastern side remained blank. Only guards on patrol with their German shepherds could go near it. What followed was a death strip with mines hidden in the sand below a raked surface so footsteps would show if somebody tried to escape. It would be a suicidal mission. Then followed a second wall with barbed wire, more guards and dogs on the ground and young men in uniform in guard towers watching the death strip with binoculars and peeping into the West. And this was where people were dancing, singing and crying now. People who had shed all fears, who had followed their cue when a party functionary misspoke, having told the press corps only hours before that travel was allowed, as of now, "unverzüglich" (without delay). He had been wrong about the new rule going into effect right there and then, but the masses could not be stopped any longer. What followed was a deluge, and the biggest party the city had ever seen.

Sitting on her bed, Iris was staring at the little TV screen. She longed to be where total strangers embraced in disbelief, leaving behind all that had been dividing them for one long, unforeseen, incredibly exciting night. Crying, silently, she chastised herself for being emotional about what she was witnessing. A nation coming together, flags being waved. "A moment in which 'hope and history rhyme'," she thought recalling the words of poet Seamus Heaney, whom she had seen on stage only a month earlier. But for her generation, nationalism was a dangerous thing, something that could be exploited, manipulated and twisted. Iris had always identified as a European first, then as German. Why then was she crying? Daniel joined her briefly, looked at the TV, but somehow did not grasp the implications of what had just happened. The Wall had fallen. The end of communism, of the Cold War. She had no-one to celebrate with.

Eager to discuss what had happened the previous night, Iris took the bus for the short ride to campus the next morning. Yet, nobody was talking, business as usual. Passengers were reading the paper, or staring out the window avoiding eye contact. Her colleagues in the office did not say anything either, met with students, prepared for classes. How could they not react to the historical earthquake that had just happened? She understood that this had more of an impact on her than on Americans, although they had thousands of troops stationed over there. Some of her colleagues finally approached her, had been unsure how this all affected her, not knowing how to bring it up. It would take people a while to adjust to the new world that was forming out there, realizing that the images on TV had consequences, sorting out how they felt about it all and what it would mean.

For Iris everything changed that night. She had not just wept because the division of her country had come to a peaceful end, but also for a future with Daniel which was not to be. She was beginning to admit to herself that they had no future. That her progress made his non-progress worse, that her tenacity made him feel weak. He had started to see a therapist, which was good for him. But this was not about saving a relationship. This was about him only.

Fifty ways to leave your lover ... Iris did not know a single one. She went home for the summer, came back to Michigan with a heavy heart, so heavy that her brother on the way to the airport asked why she was not just staying. She did not have a good answer, mentioned her job, friends in the college town, but she did not mention Daniel. In the end Daniel made the decision for her. During the summer, he had started an affair with a young, bright student who was just starting her graduate work in history, a German, of all people. Daniel did not tell her right away, but Iris felt something was wrong. His welcome at the airport was reserved. When they went swimming the next day, a hot September day, she was trying to hold on to him because she was afraid of what might be hidden in the lake's mud under her feet. He turned away avoiding her touch. She felt the pain of rejection acutely.

Though her colleagues and friends were trying to talk her into staying, and the prospects for getting a long-term contract with the writing department looked good, Iris knew that her future was not in America. She needed to go home to a changing, exciting new Germany, finish her dissertation, and build a life there. She was 32, and it was time to move on. Maybe she would be teaching about her beloved "America" in that magnificent main building of Humboldt University in the former eastern part of Berlin one day and tell her students what it had been like, the night when the Wall came down. When everything changed, even for a graduate student watching it all happen on a small TV screen in her bedroom, 7,000 miles away in a university town in Michigan. But it would take many years and a lot of waiting for Daniel to call, to tell her he missed her and wanted her to come back. He never did.

* * * * *

2021

"Whatever happened to my kitchen table?", Iris wondered decades later. "Did he schlepp it all the way across the country when he left that small Michigan university town?"

Acknowledgements

For the continued encouragement and feedback on my writing I am immensely grateful to a circle of friends (*you* know who you are) and fellow writers (see "Reviews and Comments"). I found inspiration in the profound work of American Studies' colleagues on American history and culture and the numerous readings I was privileged to organize with fabulous American writers throughout a long career.

For the chapter "Clara", I am indebted to *Women in Music: A History* edited by Karin Pendle, in particular the chapter "Women in American Music, 1800-1908" (Bloomington: Indiana University Press, 1991, 2001) by Adrienne Fried Block, assisted by Nancy Stewart. Numerous photographs and paintings of late 19th century New York to be found in books like *Die Geschichte der Deutschen in Amerika: Von 1680 bis zur Gegenwart* (Köln: Fackelträger Verlag, 2013) by Alexander Emmerlich, *Das Deutsche in New York: Eine Spurensuche* (Leipzig: Lehmstedt Verlag, 2013) by Ilona Stölken and *Spaziergänge durch New York: Historische Gemälde, Postkarten, Fotografien und Stadtpläne* (München: Bassermann Verlag, 2009) have helped me dive into the times. Brian Burt, a fellow traveler between two worlds and long-time friend from student days in Michigan, provided the finishing touch just in time with a quote from his poem "The Beginning of the End of the Beginning" published in *Black Dog Days* (Georgetown, Kentucky: Finishing Line Press, 2022).

Living in two languages has enriched my life. Adopting English as my "creative language" gave me the courage to pursue my passion for storytelling. FAMILY MATTERS wanted to be told in English first because it starts with a voice that was lost. But the book's strong rooting in a particular German region demanded its retelling in German. With PalmArtPress and Catharine Nicely, an American expat in Berlin, I have found the ideal partner to publish both versions. It was Catharine who "got me."

I am grateful to the Rheingau-based artist Michael Apitz who so creatively fused the two worlds of Elizabeth and Clara, Big Henry and Little Henry, Toni and Iris on the book cover.

Final very special thanks go to Uli, my tireless proofreader (all remaining mistakes are mine!), and Gero, the light of my life. Where would I be without you.

Aus dem Programm von PalmArtPress

Martina J. Kohl
Family Matters – *Vom Leben in zwei Welten*
ISBN: 978-3-96258-134-3
Roman, 240 Seiten, Hardcover, Deutsch

Carmen-Franceca Banciu
Ilsebill salzt nach
ISBN: 978-3-96258-130-5
Briefroman, 300 Seiten, Hardcover, Deutsch

Patricia Paweletz
Herzbruch
ISBN: 978-3-96258-131-2
Roman, 200 Seiten, Hardcover, Deutsch

Klaus Ferentschik
Ebenbild – *Agententhriller mit tiefenpsychologischer Bedeutung*
ISBN: 978-3-96258-119-0
Roman, 124 Seiten, Hardcover, Deutsch

Jennifer Kwon Dobbs
Vernehmungsraum – *Aufzeichnungen einer Vermissten*
ISBN: 978-3-96258-115-2
Lyrik, 100 Seiten, Übers. Irina Bondas, Felix Schiller, Hardcover, Deutsch

Antonio Machado
Einsamkeiten, Galerien und andere Geschichten
ISBN: 978-3-96258-117-6
Lyrik, 140 Seiten, Übers. Leo Federmair, Klappenbroschur, Deutsch

Hajo Jahn
Die Facetten des Prinzen Jussuf – *Ein Lesebuch über Else Lasker-Schüler*
ISBN: 978-3-96258-106-0
Lesebuch, 200 Seiten, Hardcover, Deutsch

Yoyo
One Man's Decision to Become a Tree
ISBN: 978-3-96258-136-7
Vier Novellen, 300 Seiten, Klappenbroschur, Englisch

Mechthild Henneke
Ach, Mein Kosovo!
ISBN: 978-3-96258-096-4
Roman, 350Seiten, Hardcover, Deutsch

Wolf Christian Schröder
Fünf Minuten vor Erschaffung der Welt
ISBN: 978-3-96258-113-8
Roman, 320 Seiten, Hardcover, Deutsch

Yang Lian
Erkundung des Bösen
ISBN: 978-3-96258-128-2
Lyrik, 90 Seiten, Hardcover, Deutsch

Peter Wortsman
Geistertanz in Berlin – *Eine Rhapsodie in Grau*
ISBN: 978-3-96258-094-0
Reise-Memoir, 164 Seiten, Hardcover, Deutsch

Fritz Bremer
Das Ungewisse ist Konkret
ISBN: 978-3-96258-112-1
Lyrik, 148 Seiten, Hardcover, Deutsch

Ilse Ritter
Weit sehe ich, weit in die Welten All – *Götterlieder der Ádda*
ISBN: 978-3-96258-074-2
Lyrik, 120 Seiten, Hardcover, Deutsch

Wolfgang Kubin
102 Sonette
ISBN: 978-3-96258-104-6
Lyrik, 128 Seiten, Hardcover, Deutsch

Fawzi Boubia
Mein West-Östlicher Divan
ISBN: 978-3-96258-114-5
Roman, 300 Seiten, Hardcover, Deutsch

MARTINA J. KOHL worked in the Cultural Section of the U.S. Embassy in Berlin, Germany, for many years. She developed and organized numerous programs, but especially loved the literature series. Writing has been a passion ever since she taught at the University of Michigan. It is part of her seminars that she teaches regularly at Humboldt University Berlin and defined her work as editor of the American Studies Journal. As an advisory board member of the Salzburg Global American Studies Program, she continues to engage in transatlantic dialogue. Among her academic publications, FAMILY MATTERS is her first novel.